GLENNA'S FUTURE

JOANNE AUSTEN BROWN

GLENNA'S FUTURE

Joanne Austen Brown

Title: Glenna's Future

Copyright © 2023 Joanne Austen Brown

BOOKS BY JOANNE AUSTEN BROWN

Always Louisa ~ Book One: Always Series

Always Elspeth ~ Book Two: Always Series

Always Delia ~ Book Three: Always Series

Rachael's Jaunt ~ Book One: Come with Me

Molly's Laird ~ Book Two: Come with Me

Glenna's Future ~ Book Three: Come with Me

NOVELLAS

The Secret Letter
A Partridge in His Family Tree
Redemption

To my readers who have loved my Time Travel. You have made this journey memorable.

THE TEAL LIGHT

"She has arrived in Duncan's time." Drake placed his hand into the queen's. The teal blue light dulled and vanished. They stood there on the hill, in the dark. For the first time in eons, he was at ease.

"Good. Glenna needs to feel she can do something to help. It is important to her and to me. After all…" The two moved slowly to the stone that stood in the centre of the hill.

"She will do so much to establish your position as queen."

"I know. It is strange I know how things will turn out, but now she does not. Glenna amazes me with her fighting spirit and her need for justice to be served. At this time, she could only guess how things would turn out. She is an amazing fae."

"She is. And we are all grateful for her input."

"True. Now she is here in 2020, we can go and observe her actions and see how she achieved her goals. It is a wonderful gift. The ability to travel in time and see how people behave. Even how they think." The queen placed her hand on the stone and smiled at Drake and continued.

"I am glad for all my family. It is not often we get back our heritage once it has been stolen. Even a heritage we didn't know we had. None of us ever thought we would be returned, even after we found out who we truly were."

"That is true. But it was rightfully yours and your ancestors."

"True. The Queen is dead. Long live the Queen."

Drake bowed and repeated the words of his queen. Soon all would be well and the balance of the fae world and that of the humans would settle and be as it should be. He took his queen into his arms. The light returned and shone, then they were gone.

BROTHER DEAR

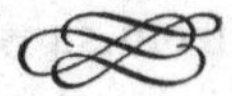

2 *020* Glenna looked around the hilltop. All was quiet. There was no sound. Not even a bird tweet. She stood there for a moment, not sure she had come to the future or was still in her own time. The sun was slowly rising. There was a light drizzle and she shivered. It was cool but she felt suddenly refreshed. She was not afraid. She moved to the edge of the hill and looked at the modern lights that shone from poles near the streets below. The black road shone as the light hit the wet black surface. She had never seen a black road before. It looked so beautiful in the dawn light. Like a long piece of jet. She was there, in the future, and would finally see her brother and Rachael again. Although she was excited to see them after a year, the main reason for her being here was to warn them. Their world and her own were not safe. That is why she had to come.

She turned and headed to the path that led to her home. The home of the future. It was there. But first she had to find her brother, now she had her bearings. She would go directly to his new home. The cottage on the estate. His new home. The path ahead was well worn and trodden.

Many came to this hill and still do.

She smiled as she made her way down the hill.

* * *

IT WAS EARLY in the morning, and she loved this time of the day. The light was so different from sunset or full sun. It was quiet with only the occasional bird welcoming in the new day. She knew she was in the future. A black road here or there where she knew there were only dirt tracks. It was strange and exciting all at the same time. Wandering on her own land, her home, made it even more special.

There on the hill was the cottage. It was a ruin of stones in her time but now a beautiful building stood in its place. The old stone she could see had been used in its construction. It put a smile on her face knowing that things went on. She gazed around at the scene in front of her. The house sat well on the hill. It was surrounded by beautiful trees and a garden of flowers. She could see herself in such a beautiful place. A smile lifted her lips and she chuckled. Duncan would be very comfortable. She went up the path.

She knocked on the cottage door. Molly had told her where her brother and Rachael were living. So, she had come straight here. And she was glad she had. The door opened and her brother Duncan stood before her. He looked strong and tall as he had always done but seeing him in modern clothing surprised her. The jeans and jumper suited him, clinging to his tall and muscular body. His hair was longer too, and it suited him also.

"Glenna. Is it really you?"

"Duncan. I had to come."

She threw herself into her brother's arms. She held on, praying she would never have to leave him again. She had missed him so.

"Glenna?"

She heard Rachael's voice and knew she was near.

Her brother pulled away gently from her hug. "Sister, are you alright? Why have you come? Are Hamish and Alasdair aware you are here? Are they with you? Are they okay?"

"Oh, Glenna it is so good to see you. Come in. How long can you stay?" Rachael pulled her into a hug.

She opened her eyes and looked at her friend Rachael and at her brother. She could feel the grin on her face getting wider and wider.

"I had to come. There is so much I need to tell you."

"Come in, come in." Duncan stood aside and she went into their beautiful home. It was warm and welcoming, and she immediately could feel the joy that existed here. She felt at home.

Rachael took her arm and led her into the lounge room. "Please sit down and tell us what is going on."

"I had to come. Molly and Sen and Alasdair…"

"Slow down sister. One thing at a time."

She closed her eyes and took a deep breath. "Yes. I am sorry. I never thought I would get the chance to see you again. I am a little overwhelmed."

Rachael sat on one side and her dear Duncan sat on the small table in front of her. He took her hands in his. He was real. Her dear brother was before her.

"Now let's start from the beginning."

She took a deep breath again and began.

"I need to tell you about Molly and her heritage."

"Molly? Who is Molly?" Duncan looked at his wife, shaking his head.

"I only found out about Molly. Last night, in fact." Rachael was shaking her head and not smiling.

"That's right. You and I are going to see Molly together for the first time soon. I should have remembered. You have not met her yet."

Duncan looked at his wife. "Do you know what she is talking about?"

Rachael nodded her head. "Molly is for Alasdair, isn't she?" She was looking at her.

"Yes. I am sorry to surprise you with this sudden visit. Let me tell you what I know. Molly is a young lady staying at Mrs. Watson's. She is from Australia, like you Rachael. She has lost all her family. To cut a long story short, the fae have been healing her on Fairy Hill. Now, in this time, but she wants to go to the past. She believes in the fae."

"And she will marry Alasdair." Her sister-in-law said, as a statement rather than a question.

"Yes. Well, I hope so. They are deeply in love. But she has just found out she is fae. In my time." She took a deep breath and continued. "This creates an issue. Her father is Sen Kalen, Stephen Kalen is Sen."

"Our farm manager?" Her brother stood and began to pace the floor.

"Yes. Seems he is also the son of Queen Sebille, queen of the fae. Which means both Molly's parents had to be fae. I want to tell you more, but it may be best to stop there. You see, Molly had no idea before she went to the past of her heritage. Now, due to the loss of her family she is the only heir."

"Why is that a problem?" Duncan asked.

"I know it is a great deal to take in. Sen's father was the rightful heir. He has passed away and Sen chose to be in the human world so rejected the throne. But we also found out Molly's mum was also distantly related to the Celeste family. She is of royal blood. That makes Molly the most obvious successor. Sen's mother, the current queen wants to destroy Sen and his family. She wants her second son to become the next king of the fae. She has had only sons."

She again paused, allowing them to absorb the information.

Duncan looked at Rachael and then back at her. Then she continued.

"Women are the rightful heirs. She wants to rid the fae world of other possible heirs. And she has a dislike of all humans, which goes against all fae belief. This queen is nothing like the fae royalty of the past."

"I understand, I think. But why have you come?"

"I want to see if the queen destroys Molly and her happiness with Alasdair. I want to make sure she does not. I need to ensure their happiness. So, I have come to read Alasdair's diaries to gain a bigger picture. And to warn you, even you could be in danger."

Rachael now stood and began to pace. And Duncan sat down.

"But this means she, the queen, could come and try to stop you."

"I know. She will probably send a fae loyal to her. A guardian or even a fae who now lives in the human world, in solitude."

"Lives in solitude?"

"A Ghillie Dhu seems the most obvious to me. Historically, they have more to do with humans. They have black hair and live in human forms but prefer their solitude. They are very hard to distinguish from humans."

"Sister, are you sure?" Duncan's concern was palpable. But he should know her better.

"Of course, I am. I know the fae. I am one, remember? I have studied fae, for many years as you know. I know their history. So, we need to be aware of anyone who is new to your acquaintance or who becomes close to you in the coming weeks. They could be fae in disguise and try to stop me."

Rachael shook her head. "Now my head is hurting. This is nuts. Here we go again." She sat down again. "Could we be in danger?"

"Yes, because I came to you and want you to help me. I want to encourage Molly to go to the past. Her life is there with Alasdair. The quicker she goes to the past the better."

"Very well, let's walk to the main house and inform the others. We need to sort this out." Duncan stood and bent down and kissed his wife.

"We do but let me make Glenna a cuppa first. And perhaps some breakfast. She has come a long way and it is still early. I also think she need to rest a while."

Duncan nodded. He seemed puzzled and she understood. He always listened to her warnings since he and Rachael got together. Even if the things she said were outrageous. And to a non-fae it would appear outrageous.

"Sounds wonderful. The cuppa, I mean. And some food would be great. Congratulations on the baby. I am so happy for you both."

Rachael stood, smiled at her, patting her tummy and left the room.

"Brother, please sit with me. I never thought I would see you again. I am so glad to be here with you."

Her brother sat down, and he took her hand.

"I am delighted to see you." Then he kissed her fingers. "Welcome home, sister. My dear feisty fae sister."

SINCLAIR

While Glenna helped Rachael clear away the breakfast dishes, Duncan pulled out his phone and called Sinclair. He already knew he must be fae. He had offered to help him in the research at the manor. He had come out of nowhere but was just who he needed for his research into the history of his family. He had thought it was too good to be true and he was right.

After the call he went into the kitchen to warn his sister.

"I believe there is a person who fits the description of intruder in our lives."

Rachael answered before he had a chance to go on. "Sinclair."

"Exactly."

"Who is he?"

"A research student from the university. He offered to help me before the lockdown was put in place. He is staying at the castle."

His sister closed her eyes. She gently nodded her head.

"Lockdown?"

"Yes, a disease is running amuck around the world."

"Yes, I remember what Molly told me. COVID. Go on."

"I have called him and asked him to come over."

"Called?"

"It is complicated. I will tell you about it later. Can your magic detect his? That is if he is fae."

"Of course. I will sense it immediately."

"Then I suggest you change into jeans and a T-shirt before he gets here. We do not want him to know you have come from the past or perhaps guess you are fae," Rachael said.

Glenna nodded.

"When you are ready, stay in the kitchen and see if you can detect if he is fae. He should be here in ten or so minutes. I will let him in."

Rachael nodded to him and took his sister's hand and led her to the bedroom where he was sure she would change clothes. He made his way back into the loungeroom and sat down, waiting for Sinclair to arrive. All of this was disturbing to him. What were the fae up to? But most of all he was angry and wanted to hit something or someone. Darn It jumped up on his lap and he immediately felt calmer.

Crazy cat.

* * *

SINCLAIR CAME into the loungeroom as Duncan closed the front door and then followed him in. He loved the little cottage and was sure Duncan did too. Being in this place always gave him a sense of peace.

"Sit down, Sinclair. We need to talk."

He sat, unsure why Duncan seemed annoyed. He was not smiling nor happy to see him. Though it was he who had asked him to come.

"Have I stuffed up the research? I was sure I was heading down the right path."

"No, Sinclair. The research is fine."

He let out the breath he had been holding. He sat back on the sofa.

"What is it? You don't seem yourself."

"I'm not. My family is in danger, and I hope you are not going to harm them."

"What…" He shuddered and sat upright; dreading Duncan had found out who he truly was.

Suddenly a tall, red headed, beautiful woman came in from the kitchen, followed by Rachael and the cat.

"I can sense the magic. He is fae. He is strong. He must be a Ghillie Dhu. Or are you a Guardian? Do not deny it?" She stared at him as if he would rise up and strike her down.

She stood there with hands on hips and legs apart. Her magic was strong too. He sensed her, more than any other fae he had come across. It was like she had a flashing neon sign on her chest which was saying 'I am fae'.

Wearing a light blue T-shirt and jeans, she looked like any other 21st century woman. But she was not. She was fae. It positively dripped out of her. He did not think she was from this time either. As for her incredible beauty… My God, she was gorgeous.

"And you are fae, too. So, what now." He stood and crossed his arms.

Duncan stood and came to tower over him. The man was so tall and intimidating. Duncan grabbed the front of his shirt.

"Explain yourself. And it had better be good."

The red-headed beauty went and sat on the couch opposite him and crossed her arms and legs. He could not keep his eyes off her.

"Sit down both of you. And you…" She pointed at him. "Explain Dhu, I am waiting."

He sat down, wiping the wrinkles of his shirt and waited for Duncan and Rachael to also sit down.

"I am Sinclair and yes, I am a Ghillie Dhu."

"Traitor. Are you here to kill me or my brother?"

His face heated. So, she was his sister. Then she had come from the past. What the hell was going on? He took a deep breath, closing his eyes for a second.

"I am not an assassin." He opened his eyes and turned to look at his tutor, Duncan, "I would never kill you or any member of your family. We are friends. Is that what you think of me?"

"That is what I thought. Except, you are fae and had not told me. What do you expect me to think?"

"That I am your friend and happen to be fae, as well as your student. But now everything feels wrong."

"Then why are you here? And why did you not reveal who you truly are?" His friend was not happy.

"I will prove to you that I am your friend. I will tell you all I know. I was sent to keep an eye on you. The queen is concerned someone evil is tracking you because you have come from the past."

"This is worse than I thought. You are working for the queen? Is that what she told you? He was in danger?" The red-headed beauty was angry.

He looked at her and nodded. "Yes. I have been in the human world for some time but when the queen came and told me of the problem, I wanted to help. Duncan is my friend and was my tutor long before the queen approached me."

Duncan's sister sighed and stood.

"The queen is the traitor. She is using you to get to me and my brother. It is complicated."

"It would seem so." He closed his eyes. He could feel her magic. It impressed him. But there was more. She was clearly telling the truth. Had the queen truly used him, and he had not known, or sensed it?

He opened his eyes and looked into the deep blue eyes of the women in front of him. Every inch of his body was alive and in tune with her. Truth was all he could see and feel. He had never experienced this with any other fae. They had a connection. He nodded.

"You believe me?" she asked.

"Yes. I cannot deny it. I feel your magic and the truth is clear in you. Please tell me what I can do to protect you and Duncan. I would never hurt any of you. It is not in my nature. But I would like to know more. I cannot believe I have been deceived by the queen."

Glenna stood there, her hands behind her and her legs apart. She looked like a warrior. She closed her eyes and announced...

"Denounce the queen before me now or leave and never come back."

He stood before her. She placed her hands on her hips. She was feisty. She demanded respect and he was happy to give it.

"I will do as you say. The queen is being dishonest. I denounce her now. Will you please tell me more? What can I do to help?"

"We will," said Duncan.

He looked at his tutor. "I am your servant and your friend. You can trust me." He bowed.

IN THE CASTLE

She and Sinclair headed out the front door and toward the castle. Rachael and her brother following behind. She needed to be cautious about this fae. She knew nothing about the real Sinclair. She wanted to know him better. But he was blocking his thoughts and that made her wary.

"You too have come to the future, like your brother."

"I have come to warn them as things are complicated at home."

They walked in silence for some time. She looked at the scenery around her. Little had changed. Trees were bigger in some places, but the feel of her home was as she knew it. The weather was the same, too. A slight drizzle in the grey sky. Ah, Scotland.

"I had been concerned the queen was behaving in an unusual way."

She looked at him. "What makes you say that?"

"We, Ghillie Dhu, love the land. We can sense more from the earth, than from fae or humans. She seemed agitated when I met with her. But as it was the first time, I had met her, I did not question her statements. We are told lying should never be part of our nature as fae. And besides, what would a queen want with a small and insignificant Ghillie Dhu?"

"You underestimate yourself and the queen. She is trying to keep the crown to herself despite not being entitled to it. She will use anyone to get what she wants."

He nodded. "Ah. But her husband was a Celeste and the last of the line?"

"She gave that impression, but we now know there are some heirs who have been in seclusion in the human world. And they have fae blood and they are the true line. And the queen wants to eliminate them."

"Why would she have me watching Duncan? Are your family the line that has been in hiding? I do not understand."

"This affects our other brother and his betrothed in the past. She is the heir."

"And that is why you have come. To let your brother know and keep an eye out for any trouble which might come his way."

"Yes. I will fill you in with all we know when we get to the castle. I will not need to repeat myself as I will be telling the family and my brother at the same time. And you should know I will be watching you to make sure you have been truthful with me."

"No problem, Glenna. May I call you Glenna?"

She looked at him again as they entered the clearing before the castle. She stopped as he did.

"How do you know my name?"

"I have been researching Duncan's family. The queen told me he was from the past. The Duncan from the past only had one sister. So, I assume you are Glenna."

"I am. And yes, you may call me by my name." She smiled and lowered her head as they continued walking. He seemed true but she still was not convinced. He was still blocking some of his thoughts.

"Thank you." He smiled at her, and she felt a little at peace. Maybe, they could be friends if that was what he really wanted.

* * *

THE AFTERNOON WAS full of discussions and plans. Later the whole family got together for dinner. It was a wonderful evening. She met descendants of her and Alasdair. Interesting, as it seemed to confirm she would return to the past. It was exhilarating and confusing all at the same time. It did make her determined to find out more.

She examined the dining room. It was similar to her home. The table and some of the chairs were the same. The painting of her parents still had pride of place over the fireplace. It was easy for her to feel like she was in her own time. Except for the people around her. Relatives she did not know.

Sinclair had listened intently to all that was revealed. But his presence disturbed her. He troubled her. He was blocking some of his thoughts. She felt it. According to him, he was tricked by the queen to keep watch. Well, she hoped so. He aligned himself to them as soon as he could. He believed in her and her magic more quickly than anyone else had ever done. She sensed his magic, and it was strong. In fact, all she could do was sense him. She was drawn to him in every way a fae and a woman could be. Not for the first time were her eyes drawn to his and she found his eyes on her.

"I agree we should let you two ladies go and meet Molly."

Her brother was right, they needed to get Molly to the past as soon as possible.

"I will call Mrs. Watson and arrange a meeting tomorrow." Rachael got up and left the room.

"I think it will be best. But it seems weird, as Rachael would say. I will be seeing her and yet she will not know we are good friends."

"Can I suggest something?"

Sinclair had been quiet for some time. His voice took her by surprise. She was drawn to his voice. Not just his magic but his voice. This seemed strange. But she shook it off. Sensing his magic was one thing, but she had yet to trust him. That would take time, despite feeling his truth.

"What do you want to suggest?" she responded.

He looked toward her.

"In your own time, you said she could sense your magic. Perhaps, I should keep my distance in case she senses my magic. I mean we do not want her to get spooked, if you know what I mean."

"I agree," Duncan added. "If she gets confused, we may be making things difficult for her. She might change her mind about going to the past."

"True. It will already be strange with me there, knowing what I know. So perhaps you should stay out of sight at least for now." She looked at Sinclair.

"That can be easily achieved. I will stay in the library and continue the research. Just don't let her wander the castle alone. Please."

"Great idea." She paused for a moment. "Duncan, can I use Sinclair to help me with what I need to know from the diaries?"

"Good suggestion. It will be useful if he starts on the diaries of the time you are looking into." Duncan smiled at her.

"And when I return tomorrow, I can help with the search."

"That is settled. Perhaps we should call it a night. And Glenna, your room will be available here. While you are at Mrs. Watson's tomorrow, Sinclair can help me move us all into the big house. I will feel safer if Rachael and I are here. So, when you get back you can both start together on the diaries."

She sensed in her brother the concern of a non-family member looking at his prized possessions, Alasdair's diaries. She disliked the fact she could see into others and their motives. It was not always comfortable. But what disturbed her more was the fact she could sense Sinclair's magic but not all his thoughts. What was he thinking? What was he hiding? This was making it hard to trust him.

* * *

WHAT SHE HAD LEARNED of this disease which was running rampant in the world only made her more concerned and confused. She worried mostly about Rachael and her unborn baby. Would they and Duncan be safe? This disease was something she had never contemplated for their future. It would seem there was no real safe place in any time. Having a doctor in the family eased her concerns somewhat, and she was sure being in the big house all together would be more beneficial in the long run. Especially if the lockdown continued.

"Here is a mask." Rachael handed her a blue and white mask which seemed to be made from some kind of paper. She stared at it. She watched Rachael place it on her face and she did the same.

"How can something so flimsy protect us?"

"You would be surprised. But we need to be seen wearing it while we are out, in the eyes of other people. Everyone is scared. No one knows who to trust. I suggest you wear it while you are in the castle wandering around. If you are alone in your room, then you can leave it off. And you must change it every day."

"I will do as you say."

"Once Dr. Peter's gets a vaccine, we should be better prepared. Beside you won't be seeing many more people, just family."

"I would love to have a good look around, but I understand why I cannot. And besides I am sure I will return to my own time soon enough. After all, I had dinner with some of my future descendants." She giggled. "This is so very unusual."

Rachael laughed. "It is weird, very weird. Will you go back soon?"

"I think I must, if only to see we are on the right track. I might not need to come back. We will see."

"Maybe then we can show you around. I would love you to see how Scotland was doing. Especially, all the things I suggested you introduce to the estate."

"I am sure your ideas will do well. Perhaps it is for the best. Too much knowledge of the future could be damaging."

SEEING MOLLY

They had their face masks on when Molly came into the room. She and Rachael stood to greet her. At this moment she was glad she had the mask to hide behind. She wanted to see Molly as if she was seeing her for the first time. After the initial introductions, Rachael suggested they take the masks off, so she did. But they kept a good distance away from her friend. She did all in her power to keep a straight face in a hope she would not reveal anything unnecessarily. In her head were Rachael's words, 'this is weird'.

She listened and watched Rachael speak to Molly with ease. This all felt so strange. After all, she knew Molly and should be calm and relaxed. But she was not. Molly had to go back to the past and she was terrified she would say or do something wrong which might change Molly's mind. Mrs. Watson soon left and went to get tea.

Glenna concentrated her thoughts on Molly as she told her story. A story she had heard before. Molly's sadness and loss was real, and it showed on her face with tears, downturned lips and an ever-present feeling of guilt, that she was still alive, and her family was not. She listened to her descriptions of what happened to her family. Her dismissiveness toward her father. A man that soon would re-enter her life. Hearing the words she had heard before. Everything was going to be so much better for her once she came to the past.

Molly made a comment about her brother Duncan being good looking, and she answered, "That is perfectly acceptable. I am just surprised you had time to notice." She tuned back into the conversation.

Oh yes, Molly was for Alasdair. Seeing her open up like this again was another remarkable experience. Rachael had brought up her belief in the fae and how the hill had been healing Molly. Her magic was strong and clear at this point. It took away any doubt that still may have been hidden in the back of her mind. Not that she had any, but the fact Molly believed was itself magical. She walked over to Molly and took her hand.

In a more relaxed mood, she added, "Your heart will heal."

* * *

RACHAEL and she spent hours together talking with Molly. But finally, they headed back to the castle. For now, her aim was to get back to the past as soon as she could. Once she was sure of the future for her brother and Rachael, and that of Molly and Alasdair, she could return to the past.

The diaries became her next objective. Hopefully, what they needed to know was in the diaries Alasdair kept for his brother and Rachael. Over the coming days, she and Sinclair spent hours and hours reading entries in the year after Duncan had left. At least she knew Molly and Alasdair would marry and that made her less stressed. He wrote of Molly's fae heritage sparingly at least till 'the event'. The day Molly stood up for herself. Her wedding day.

A bonus was getting to know Sinclair as they worked. She found him both helpful and determined, regarding the truth for her in the diaries. Talking to him helped her relax about the fae queen. She was sure Sinclair did not want to help the queen in any way. But he was still blocking some of his thoughts. That disturbed her. However, it was nice to have him sitting next to her. There seemed to be a definite connection between them.

"I can't believe she manipulated me." He was gently shaking his head from side to side.

"I believe the guardians, overall, felt the same way. They were shocked to think the queen would want them to turn on another fae. And commit murder if necessary."

"I understand what they might feel like. I know we Ghillie Dhu are quiet and tend to stay alone, but I had no idea she would use our nature against us, against me, and to further her own position. That is not how the fae do things. We support humans and those fae who wish to become part of the human world. It has always been like that."

She gently laid her hand on his right arm. She could feel his energy pulsating into her hand. His magic was strong, but she could not sense all his thoughts. Did he really want to protect her and her brother? Let alone Molly. She wanted him to understand what the magic meant to her. Maybe then he could see the truth and she could sense all his thoughts. She took her hand away. Her thoughts turned inward as she spoke.

"My mother was fae and she loved my father who was human. Enough to give up being fae to be with him." She paused and looked at Sinclair. He seemed to be paying attention. "She wanted to stay with him and raise a family. I have Duncan and two other brothers in the past. My mother adored all of us. I do know from my brothers—my mother was delighted when I was born. She wanted a daughter to share her stories about the fae and to one day be fae. She had taken Hamish into her confidence already not sure she would ever have a daughter. He always believed her tales and passed many on to me. You see, my mother passed away when I was still quite young. Hamish helped me to obtain the knowledge I needed about the fae as I grew. He, in some respects stood in for my mother."

"I have no memory of my parents. I understand they were both fae. When I was old enough, I chose to be Ghillie Dhu. I have no regrets until now." He was looking beyond her. He was distant. Far away but still she could not sense what he was thinking.

"What do you mean?" He turned and she looked into his indigo eyes.

"I may tell you some time, but I want to think about what you have told me about the guardians and the queen before I decide. It would seem our world is not what it once was and that makes me very sad."

"You are being very mysterious. And sound so serious." She sensed his doubt.

"Yes and no, it is just my nature."

She nodded and they continued to read the diaries. But her eyes drifted toward him regularly. The truth. She had to find the truth.

* * *

NEVER HAD he wanted to spend time with another fae. It went against his usual nature. He was Ghillie Dhu. They were loners. But being with Glenna was both a unique experience and a scary one. He had feelings for her. He was attracted to her as a woman but also as a fae. He liked her and wanted to be in her company. Talking with her was informative and exciting. Hearing the stories of her family enthralled him. Everything about her was opening feelings he did not know he had. He could not stop thinking about her. But he had to keep his thoughts from her. Because he could not have these feelings. He was Ghillies Dhu. And he did not want to scare her.

Reading about her in the past also captivated him. Although

she was the youngest of her family, she held respect and authority with her siblings. It had to be because she was fae. Like him. Though no one held him in great reverence. Often, he would close his eyes and imagine her in the past.

Nearly every day they would go together for a long walk around the estate. Through the woods, to the stables, toward the fields and near the cottage where Duncan and Rachael lived. Of course, they were living in the castle now. So, they often dropped in to see Darn It, Duncan and Rachael's cat. He was very fond of this mysterious cat. He was a sleek grey tall cat. He had seen the photos of Darn It as a kitten, 'a bundle of fluff' Rachael called him. But now he had grown into a handsome kitty.

He reached for the key on top of the door frame and opened the door.

"Darn It?"

The cat opened his eyes from the sofa where he was laying. He imagined the kitty smiling as he and Glenna came into the living room.

"Hey, Darn It." Glenna made her way to the sofa and began to pet the grey bundle. "You are a spoilt wee man." She giggled.

"What is funny?"

"Oh, I am remembering how my brother calls Alasdair my 'wee man' because he is slightly taller than him."

"You love your family deeply." It was a statement because it was true.

"Of course." She looked at him, her eyes questioning him. He closed his thoughts to her. "Why do you ask?"

"It is just not what I am accustomed to seeing. That is all."

"Sinclair, you cannot fool me. It is much more than that. What concerns you?"

"I honestly am not sure."

"Really?"

"Yes. Family interactions are not what I am used to. I am

unsure of the usual behaviors or what I should think in those situations." He came over and started to pat Darn It.

Darn It stretched and rubbed up against his hand.

"Here is an interaction that can be considered family like. Darn It likes you."

"Darn It likes a pat."

"Well, I think it is more. He has been very selective in who he allows to pat him. He thinks you are part of the family, obviously. Rachael says he is very particular."

He looked down at the cat who was looking up at him. He could not help himself and smiled at the feline. Darn It stared back at him then placed his front paws on his body and was suddenly in his arms. The cat began to rub up against his face. He could almost tear up at this silly little reaction from a cat he had grown to like over the previous months. Sinclair sat on the sofa and continued to pat him.

Glenna sat next to him.

"He has stirred my emotions. I cannot deny it. Silly cat."

"Consider his attempts at friendship a real indication of affection. He likes you."

He sat back and the cat settled on his lap and went to sleep. He chuckled to himself.

"What makes you chuckle?"

"That I could have family connections even with a cat."

"I am sorry you know nothing of your real family, and you have been alone for so long. I cannot imagine being without my brothers. I have missed Duncan this past year and am so glad I have had the chance to spend more time with him."

"I am pleased for you. As for me, it is what I am used to and have been made for."

"Made for? Can you not choose a different path?"

"I am Ghillie Dhu."

"Do you always have to be?"

For the first time in his life, he asked himself that question.

Did he want to be Ghillie Dhu? Could he be a fae who has chosen to be different? Could he want to be with others? He wanted to be with Glenna, but he doubted he would ever have the chance to be with her, other than the time they have now.

"Thank you, Glenna. You have given me much to think about."

"You are welcome." She stood and headed toward the kitchen. "You just enjoy Darn It's company while I make us a cup of tea." And she stepped into the kitchen.

He patted the cat, thinking about what a family would look like. Could he have one? Did he really have to be alone for the remainder of his life?

* * *

"I MEANT to ask you about Molly. How did your visit go with her?"

She placed her mug on the coffee table and leaned back onto the sofa.

"It went well but felt very strange and unreal."

He looked at her and smiled. Every time he looked at her, her stomach did a somersault. He affected her as no one else had. She liked him. Could it be more than that? It was silly of her to even question herself. The men of her time she had no feelings for. Her brothers' friends could not capture her attention let alone her imagination. But in a very short time this fae, who was not revealing all his thoughts to her, had captured her.

"Molly will be for Alasdair. I know that. In fact, I knew she would before I even arrived in this time. But watching her now and waiting for her to go back, has me on tenterhooks. Will all go well?"

"I think I understand, and I am sure we will be able to find out more in the diaries. I guess we should head back." He looked down at Darn It who was fast asleep. "Will you still be my friend if we leave you and head back to the castle?"

She laughed out loud. "See you care for him more than you know."

He picked him up and placed him on the warm spot where he had been sitting. Darn It stretched and curled back up into a ball and slept on.

"I think I am forgiven."

GETTING TO KNOW YOU

They made their way back to the castle and into the library to continue their search. He did enjoy their time together. Being with her now made him glad to be here. What the queen was doing was wrong. He could understand now. He held his breath as he looked at Glenna. Back and forth his gaze went to her. Could Glenna sense the truth in him? Could she see he was right? It was late in the afternoon when he came across something which he was sure she wanted. Now, as he read through more of the diaries. What he has found was very interesting. Could this be what she was looking for?

"Listen to this....

A group of guardians showed up this morning. On our wedding day. They wanted to try to stop us from getting married. Molly was regal. If I needed proof, she was fae, I saw it firsthand. She made it clear she did not want to go to the fae domain. Nor did she accept she was an heir to the throne. She chose me and the life we wanted together here on earth and in this time. The love I have for this woman transcends everything else I have ever experienced.

We are determined that nothing will keep us from the life we want to lead. Nothing.

This is amazing."

"So, this is what the guardians are up to. They want Molly for their queen. That will put Molly in danger as the current queen is still alive and looking for her. We need to see Molly and encourage her to go to the past as soon as she can. She needs Alasdair and he needs her."

Glenna sat back and sighed. This seemed to be a turning point. With Alasdair's own words ringing in her ears, she had to agree with what Sinclair had just read aloud.

"They were married that day. The guardians did not stop them." He brought his gaze up from the diary and looked into her eyes.

"You are right. We need to encourage her to go and soon. I will talk with Rachael and Duncan. Thank you, Sinclair. This is what we needed. I will need to go back to the past and warn Molly. But not just yet. I think we need to keep reading and see if there is anything else."

"I will be happy to do so. But can I suggest a break for a while? We have been searching for days and could do with the break. Can I suggest a walk in the woods?"

"That would be a wonderful idea. Though we did have a walk this morning. Darn It enjoyed our appearance if you remember." She started to laugh. "Who cares? Come on."

* * *

THEY HEADED out over the open space in front of the castle. And went further left and toward the wood.

"This must be strange for you as a Ghillie Dhu. You are alone for most of your life."

He turned his head to look at Glenna. The afternoon sun glowed through the red of her hair. Beautiful. "Yes, we tend to be alone. I do not find it uncomfortable though. I do enjoy spending time with humans. I have not known many fae."

"You knew Duncan was in part fae, did you not?"

"Only because the queen had told me. I did not sense any magic. To me, he had no obvious gifts. Now, I know he is not fae but born of fae. But he and I have similar interests, history for one, so we enjoy each other's company."

"I did notice a connection between you. You really are friends."

"I view him as a friend. Despite my revelation as to who I am. I also believe we still are." He thought for a moment. "Well, at least I hope so."

"I agree. Duncan likes you and I believe he trusts you again. You have laid your cards on the table, you could say."

"Yes. I had no idea the fae world was in such turmoil. We, Ghillie Dhu, tend to immerse ourselves in the human world and that can be difficult enough. But this disturbance…"

They walked into the trees with few words passing between them. The last words he spoke hung in the air around them. The light hit the leaves and the filtered light drifted around him. Being close to Glenna made him wonder what living with another fae would be like. He wanted to ask her but doubted he could put the words together. She captivated him in a way he could not fathom. He was out of his comfort zone.

"What of Molly? Do you think she is right for Alasdair?"

"Most definitely. She is sweet and kind and sad all at the same time."

"Sad because she has no one?"

"She has a new family now, or will when she goes back, but she still misses those she has lost. Her mother and her sister and niece. She will grieve them all her life." She was defensive. Her love for Molly was clear.

"I think I understand…" He pondered over her words.

"Have you not lost family?"

"I have always been alone. I have no memory of my family. A mother or father. Or siblings. I have always been alone. Just me."

"I am sorry to hear that. I love my brothers and now my sister-in-law and my soon-to-be sister-in-law, Molly. I do not imagine life without them. I wish you could experience those feelings."

"Why?"

"Because it will make you a better fae."

That took him by surprise. He had never heard a fae speak of the benefits you could receive from being around humans. Only that they enjoyed their company. She was giving him a great deal to think upon.

"Oh, did I tell you I spoke briefly to Rachael after lunch. Molly is moving into the castle to prepare for her trip back in time."

"Okay. I will need to stay out of her way."

"You do not want her to sense you."

"I do not. I will talk to Duncan about staying out of her way."

She smiled. "I have enjoyed spending time with you."

"And I you. And we still have time until you go back."

"True. And there are more diaries."

"As a Ghillie Dhu, I don't believe I am going to say this." He paused and looked deeply into her eyes. Eyes that were fixed on him. "Glenna, I would like to get to know you more. Will you spend more time with me? While you can?"

She looked at him.

"Yes, Sinclair. I would like to know more about you. I would love to spend more time with you."

* * *

AT DINNER that evening Sinclair and she shared with the family what they had discovered in the diaries. Everyone agreed that Sinclair should stay out of Molly's way until she had gone.

"Can I suggest Duncan, that I stay at your cottage. I can look after Darn It. I will take some diaries with me, and Glenna can come and replace them as needed. And Molly will have no reason to come to the cottage as you will be here in the castle."

"I think it is a wonderful idea. I would feel better knowing Darn It has some company. And perhaps you can do a few jobs for me?" Rachael was beaming.

"I would be happy to. What do you have in mind?"

"The nursery needs to be painted. I want it to be the palest of blues. The cot needs to be put together and a few other things."

"I could do that. Make a list and I will do all I can."

Duncan was smiling and he was nodding at his friend. The trust was back between them. She could sense it. But she still had doubts and did not want to tell her brother. Sinclair was still blocking some of his thoughts and that disturbed her. But everything else suggested he was totally on their side. She would need to keep an eye on him. Now he had asked to get to know her better, she could visit him at the cottage and observe him in close quarters. Perhaps then she could break through his blocked thoughts.

"Can I suggest Sinclair keep studying the diaries in case we have missed any important development. I will stay a while longer and then go back."

The doctor spoke up. "I should have the first of the tests to see if you have COVID. We can test you before you go. I will also suggest that if you have any symptoms, you isolate yourself when you get back. I will write out all you need to do and give that information to you."

The lights dimmed, and a teal green hue filled the air around them. Two men were standing in their midst.

"We need to speak with Glenna."

Duncan and Sinclair were on their feet immediately as were some of the other men in the family.

"Who the hell are you?" her brother demanded.

Glenna stood. "They are the guardians. And it would seem they have followed me here. Am I right?"

"We are, Miss Glenna. I am Blake and this is my brother. His name for now is not important."

Glenna looked at Sinclair.

"Well, you are not a guardian."

"I am not. I told you I am Ghillie Dhu. I did not lie to you."

She turned her head back to the guardians. "You cannot stop me."

"We do not want to stop you, Glenna. We are here to confirm a few things. We, like you, believe the queen is acting outside her authority and against fae law." Blake placed his hands behind his back waiting for her response.

"I am pleased to hear what you have learned. Then I must return to my own time and warn my family."

"We ask you to warn them but not give specifics."

"Why should I do that?"

"We can promise you no one will die. But we need the queen to think she has won so we can catch her."

"But will my family get hurt?"

"Not permanently."

"That is unacceptable. I will not have any harm come to them."

Sinclair stepped in front of Blake. "I will tell you what you need to know."

Glenna grabbed his arm and swung him to her. "You will do no such thing. This is my family. You cannot play with their lives."

"Glenna, please understand…" he stuttered.

"No, I will not listen. I knew you were keeping something from me. You wish to harm us. Do not lie to me."

"I am not lying. I want the queen to be captured and all this come to an end. I want you all protected and in no danger. You, Molly, and Duncan."

"Blake, I suggest you and I and Sinclair discuss this in private."

Her brother looked at her, pleading with his eyes for her to remain quiet. She did not.

"And what of me? Do I not have a say in the proceedings? After all I came to warn you and save Molly and Alasdair."

Duncan came and stood before her. Her nostrils flared as she glared at Duncan standing in front of her. Glenna's eyes were narrowed and her lips were pressed together in a thin line. Her hands were clenched into fists, and she was shaking with anger. She could feel the heat rising in her face, and she knew that she was seconds away from exploding. Everyone else were silent, and all she could hear was the big clock ticking loudly from the hall. She took a deep breath and tried to calm down, but it was no use. She was too angry. She opened her mouth to say something, but she couldn't find the words. She just stood there, trying not to shake with rage. Why did he always have to be the big brother?

"I only want to help our family. You must know that? I will not let anything bad happen to them," Duncan pleaded.

"But they have magic." She pointed to the guardians. "They might lie. Just like the queen is lying."

He placed his hand on her upper arms to gain her full attention.

"The fae do not lie. We know that."

She was shocked. It was true. It was believed the fae do not lie but she never expected to hear those words come from her brother.

"I thought so, too. But the queen has been lying and him, the Ghillie Dhu, has been hiding things from me."

"Glenna, is that all I am, a Ghillie Dhu? I have not lied to you."

"No, but you are blocking some of your thoughts. Do not deny it."

"I won't deny it. I am blocking my thoughts of you. I like you, maybe even love you. But I do not want to scare you. We, Ghillie Dhu, are loners as you well know. These feelings are new for me. So, I have been blocking them."

She stared at him. Love. Her forehead creased in pain as she looked at all the family gathered around her. She rubbed her temples, trying to massage away the ache. She could feel the tension building in her head, and she knew that she was about to have a headache. She closed her eyes and took a deep breath, trying to calm herself down. Glenna didn't want to make another scene, but she didn't know how much longer she could hold on. She finally opened her eyes and looked around the room. Everyone was staring at her, and she could feel the heat rising in her face. She turned and fled the room, hoping that the fresh air would help her headache.

WHAT NOW?

*G*lenna lay on the bed, her body curled up in a ball. Her face was buried in her pillow, and her sobs racked her body. The tears had been flowing for hours, and she was exhausted. She had been crying so much that her eyes were swollen and her throat was sore. She didn't know how much longer she could keep going. She thought about him and how he had betrayed her family. She felt betrayed and heartbroken. What was she going to do?

How could Sinclair do that to her if he loved her as he said he did. And how can her brother keep her from the discussions with the guardians? Especially, when only she could tell what their magic was doing. She had no respect. She felt no respect. Coming here had been a stupid mistake.

There was a tap at her door.

"Come in."

Rachael put her head around the door.

"Can't sleep?"

"How can I knowing I have been betrayed by my own brother?"

"Betrayed? No." She came into the room and sat on the end of her bed.

"He totally excluded me from the discussions with the guardians. Yet I am fae and he is not."

"That is a bit unfair, don't you think?"

"How on earth can you see that as unfair? He usurped my position."

"You were extremely upset with Sinclair and what he had said. You were angry and distressed. Could you have thought straight for a few minutes, let alone deal with the guardians?"

Glenna pulled herself up into a seated position. She was angry and distressed with Sinclair. Perhaps, she had been a bit rash to include her brother in her anger.

"Have they sorted things out?" Her tone was full of sarcasm.

"They are still talking. I thought you might want to go and talk with them."

"Not if Sinclair is with them. He is the one who betrayed me."

"Perhaps. He was only keeping his feelings from you."

"No, he is telling them what I do not want them to know, to trap a queen who has killing and death on her mind."

"True. But the guardians have promised not to allow any death to occur to our family members."

"But, can we trust them? And what if they are not family? Alasdair might lose the love of his life or a child they might bear. Or someone close to them at the time."

"The guardians have made it clear they will protect our family. They are mine, too. I would be screaming at the top of my lungs if I thought anyone would be seriously hurt."

"But what if someone does get hurt? I do not think I could forgive myself."

"All of us could get hurt at any time. Duncan and I came back from the past and landed straight into a serious pandemic. We can only do what we can do. Even with your insight you can't prevent any of us getting hurt. Perhaps we need to trust the guardians in this matter."

"Perhaps." She got up and brushed her hair then went into her ensuite and washed her face.

"Try to trust, Glenna, please? For your own sake."

"I will try. You are right. Thank you, Rachael. You are my family, too."

* * *

She knocked on the library door.

"Come." She heard the muffled voice of Duncan.

She stepped into the room. Duncan was seated on the sofa as was the current laird, also named Duncan. The guardians were seated on the floor in front of the open fire.

"Glenna, please come in." Her brother stood.

The guardians both stood as well. She sat down on the other sofa opposite her brother. She kept her head down and her eyes fixed to the floor.

"What have you decided?" She was reluctant to hear what they had come up with without her. The guardians sat down again as did her brother.

Blake was first to speak. "We will not decide until we have heard your thoughts on the matter."

"I thought my words did not matter."

The nameless guardian spoke directly to her. "On the contrary, Miss Glenna, your opinion matters greatly to us. We know you only want what is best for your family and for the fae. You do not have any ulterior motives."

"Does the Ghillie Dhu?"

"He does not trust the queen and wants to keep your family safe."

"Huh."

Duncan sighed. "You know he tells the truth. Sinclair wants to do what is right. The fact he has feelings…"

"We do not need to discuss him anymore." She had spoken with much more force than she had intended. She shook her head and they continued.

"We wish to offer Molly the chance to connect with her heritage. We wish to offer her the chance to be queen."

"She will not take it. She loves Alasdair."

"We know, but we want the current queen to learn of the offer."

She stood up and held her hands tight to her body. She was so mad.

"If you do that, Queen Sebille will try and kill her."

"She may. But we will protect Molly."

"You say you will protect her but what has happened to her family? Did you protect them?"

"They died as fate required. We had no hand in it nor did the queen. As you are aware, we do not kill."

"But, Queen Sebille will kill. Despite being fae, she has vowed to kill Molly, has she not?"

"Please Glenna, sit down."

She did. But her jaw clenched. Glenna could feel the heat rising in her chest. She took a deep breath, trying to calm down, but it was no use. Her anger was like a fire burning inside of her, and it was getting harder to control. She could feel her face getting hotter and hotter.

The guardian continued. "Perhaps she will try but we will not allow her to succeed. The fae are watching over her as we speak. Molly's own father has taken on the role of guardian to protect his daughter."

"What am I to do? Say nothing. Pretend like none of this could happen?"

"No. Warn them but stop reading the diaries so you cannot

warn them of further actions that will come. It is up to us not to change what is to come."

"Can you guarantee no one will die?"

"You can be assured they will not. Not until age and infirmity takes them."

"Very well. I will take you at your word. I will return to the past as soon as I can. But be warned. If anyone dies, I will come and find you. Wherever you go, no matter how long it takes. I will find you."

"We understand, Glenna. We will keep them safe."

The two guardians stood and the teal light they had seen before appeared around them and they were gone. But her anger remained.

Laird Duncan stood. "I think you need to speak to each other. It has been an eventful evening. I'm tired. Good night." He smiled at them as he left the room.

"Good night, Duncan."

Her brother got up and came and sat next to her. "You thought I would let them do as they wished."

"Yes. I thought you doubted my abilities."

"Never. But I did see the shock on your face when Sinclair said what he said."

The tears she had thought had dried up began to flow again. "He betrayed me."

"My dear sister. I do not think he did. He wanted to protect you. I think he has very deep feelings for you."

She looked at Duncan and gently shook her head. She could not believe him. "How could he?"

"Easily, sister. He has deep feelings. Imagine what must be going on in his mind. He is Ghillie Dhu. They are loners. They do not have mates. They are fae that stay separated from their own kind and live in the world of humans. But Sinclair does not feel like that anymore. His thoughts go against all he has known."

"You seem to know a lot about it. I thought the fae meant little to you."

"That is not so. I have done much study and asked many questions of the guardians, Sinclair, and even Hamish, before I came here. Your abilities given to you by our mother have astonished me. But it is my heritage, too."

She looked at him and slowly grinned. Then she became serious. She reached out and took his hand.

"How can he feel that way for me? He is, as you say, Ghillies Dhu. It makes no sense."

"Perhaps. But I saw him the moment he saw you. I know love when I see it. Almost immediately I saw Rachael, I fell in love. I believe Sinclair has done the same with you, my little sister."

"I do not think so."

"I believe I said the same thing to you—when I loved Rachael and you pointed it out to me."

* * *

Glenna went to her bedroom but could not sleep. Well after midnight, she sat up and called Blake's name. The teal light appeared as did Blake.

"I came immediately. I could sense you would call me."

"I want to go back. I want to be with you when we make Alasdair and Molly aware of her being heir. I know in my heart she will reject your offer. I just want to be there to help her."

"Very well. Meet us on the fairy hill before dawn and we will go back with you."

The teal light appeared again and was gone and so was Blake.

She got up and wrote some notes. One for Duncan and Rachael telling them of her need to go back and be with Molly and Alasdair. She said she might come back but doubted it.

She went and saw the doctor who used the test to see if she had COVID. She was sorry to get him out of bed. But he assured her he did not mind and understood what she had to do. He gave her a note telling her what she must do should she feel unwell.

She came back to her room and wrote one more note. This one was for Sinclair, begging him to do no more research on the diaries. She said nothing of his revelation, nor that she may ever come back. She changed into the clothes she came in, and made her way quietly out of the castle.

A WEDDING

August 1823

At dawn, Blake and his nameless brother met her on fairy hill. They came back to the day she knew would be Molly and Alasdair's wedding day. The guardians went ahead of her. When she arrived in the past, she was alone on the hill. But she knew she would see Blake and his brother again soon.

She walked to the castle, went in and was standing outside the library. She could hear men talking. She knew the fae were in there discussing Molly's future. Her brother Hamish came down the stairs and hugged her.

"I am glad you are here."

"As am I."

She heard the raised voice of whom she assumed was a guardian. It was not the voice of Blake. Perhaps it was Jake, another brother, of whom Blake spoke. It did not sound like his nameless brother.

"…we rule this land. Laird, you have no say."

She swung open the door.

"But I do. I am the family's fae representative, you could say, and you need to hear what I have to say." She could feel the hand of her brother on her back, letting her know he was there to help her, if needed.

But Blake was there, and she knew he too would force this other guardian, his brother, to heed her words.

She turned to speak with him. "Blake, you have seen the evidence and the proof of the decision Molly will make. She will not go to the fae. She will stay with Alasdair. Can we not leave them to the life they want?"

Blake looked at Glenna and she could see his slight smile.

"The queen has been stripped of her powers and is in the year 2098. She can do no damage. For her, it is over. But we need a queen."

"But it is not Molly, nor should it be. She has not known she was even fae until a matter of weeks ago." Surely, Blake understood this?

"I agree. Molly is my love. She does not want anything from the fae, other than to stay here in the past." Her brother Alasdair was ready for a fight, and she knew he would if he had too, regardless of the fact they were fae.

Blake placed his hands behind his back. "I understand. But it is a question I need as guardian to put to her. I need to hear it from her lips so we can go and put in place plans until an heir comes forth."

"Blake. You came to me years ago and did not ask that question of Carina?" Sen seemed angry.

"Because she would not accept, she was fae. She never did. You know Molly has accepted she is fae. I now must ask the question."

Molly came in through the open door and everyone stopped talking. The air was filled with little lights reflecting off the gems on her wedding dress.

Glenna couldn't take her eyes off of her future sister-in-law. She was so beautiful, and she could sense her kindness and caring nature.

"Blake?" Molly whispered. "Ask the question."

"Your majesty." The three men bowed.

"Ask the question please, Blake." Her voice was a little louder but in her control.

"Will you, Molly, become the queen of the fae?"

"I recognise the importance of the question. No, I will not. I love Alasdair Murray and wish to marry him and stay here in the past." Glenna breathed a sigh and smiled broadly. Molly was majestic, standing tall and showing her confidence by smiling a Mona Lisa smile. She was making her position clear.

"Very well, your highness. We will depart." The three men bowed.

"No. Please stay, for the wedding. Then there will be no doubt as to the decision I have made. I do not want anyone else coming to me, to change my mind. Do you understand? There will be no more fae visits."

All three fae bowed again and went to the back of the room.

Glenna watched as her brother, Alasdair, stepped forward. "Molly dearest, will you marry me?"

"I thought you would never ask."

He took her hand and led her out into the garden. Everyone from the library followed them out.

The day was cloudy but there was no sign of rain. They walked to the great oak tree in the far garden. Other guests, clan members and staff came from everywhere. In minutes all were gathered under its boughs.

The pastor of the Kirk in the Square, in the village, stepped forward and stood in front of Molly and Alasdair.

"There is going to be a wedding."

From the battlements of the castle a lone piper began to play, and the sun poked its way out of the clouds. She was home and would finally witness the joy she had wanted for her brother and for Molly.

* * *

WHAT A GLORIOUS DAY. To see her brother and Molly wed was wonderful. All her family and her clan together to see the momentous event of the laird and his lady being joined together. She watched Blake and his unnamed brother and other brother Jake see for themselves the great event. Before the food came out, Blake came to her.

"We can see she respects the magic and the fact she is fae. I understand the love she has for Alasdair. She has chosen for the best."

"I agree. She wants Alasdair and life with him is more important."

Blake bowed as did the nameless brother.

Jake looked at her and a shiver went up her back. He did not look happy, and he also did not get his way.

"They love each other, Jake." She looked deep into his eyes. "You must understand."

He said nothing but bowed and walked away.

The worst had to be over. They were alive and together, Molly and Alasdair. The queen was supposedly arrested in the future. She had to hope life for all of them would be better. Sinclair came into her thoughts. She shook her head and went to enjoy more of the glorious day.

WHAT WILL I DO NOW?

For days she tried to settle back into her life, here where she knew she had to be. But Sinclair kept creeping into her thoughts. How could a fae who had kept his feelings from her, stay in her thoughts? She had enjoyed doing research with him. But he hid things from her, and she was not sure she could ever forgive him. But that was immaterial. He was in the future, and she was here in the past. And that was that.

He stayed in her mind. And so did the possibilities of accidents that might occur to Alasdair and Molly. What should she do? Where should she stay? Was her life here in the past or back in the future? She could not make up her mind. So, she decided to talk with Alasdair. After all, it was their lives she was concerned about.

This morning the whole family would have breakfast together. She was to meet with Alasdair after that. She thought she had worked out what to do but a discussion with him would determine it.

"I am so glad you came, Father," Molly said to her da.

"I am happy to be here and very thankful. My life is complete now that you have come." Sen replied.

Molly smiled at her father.

"And may I ask what about your new family members?" She waited patiently to hear her answer.

"Well, you know I am so pleased you are back. You are my dearest friend not just my sister-in-law."

"But I might return to the future for a short period of time. But I will come back. My future is here, I think." She loved her home in this period of time. She was happy here. There was less complication. Perhaps Sinclair might come here… She believed she would come back.

"I am pleased to hear that. Are you able to share what happened when you went to the future?"

"I will but not yet. A few things need to be…completed." More than anything she wanted to tell Molly what was going on. But had decided to tell Alasdair first. She did not want to scare Molly. She was so happy and wanted her to remain so.

"It is all very mysterious."

"Well, that's normal," Hamish added. "It would not be Glenna if it was not so. Am I not right, brother?"

Alasdair was chuckling. "Yes, you are right."

"I will miss you until you return. When do you plan to leave?" Molly asked.

"Soon. I will let you know when I go. If I go." Glenna lowered her head. Maybe her discussion with her brother would help her decide.

"And you, Hamish? When do you plan to head back to Edinburgh?" Alasdair asked him.

"Well, I will help Molly make a list of things she wants for the house and then I will go and have them ready for when you come down to the city." He gave his brother a knowing grin.

"I am so excited to be going. To see your businesses and all you have achieved. I have some ideas I hope can be added to your holdings. Just my contribution to the family's fortunes."

"I look forward to hearing all about them as we walk around

the house this afternoon. We can compare yours and Rachael's."
Hamish added.

"And be sure brother, she has whatever she wants."

"Thank you, dearest. It will be measured but needed items."

"I am sure, my dear. Glenna and I have some discussions
also. So…"

He stood, leaned down, and kissed Molly and left the room.

Glenna followed, a smile lifting her lips. Everyone was so
happy.

"That will be an interesting morning and conversation."

Molly laughed.

"I heard that," Glenna called back to them. And the laughing
echoed as she followed her brother down the hall.

* * *

"It is so strange for me. I usually have no problem making
decisions. But now I do not know what to do." She was leaning
back onto the sofa, staring at her brother.

He probably thinks I am crazy.

"Well, I am glad you came back when you did. Not just to be
there for the wedding but to support Molly as she told the
guardians what she was going to do. Do you love him?"

"I do not know. I am attracted to him."

"Think. Do you love him?"

"He affects me like no other fae, or man has. Perhaps I do."

"All of us were smitten, you might say, when first we met our
other halves. Remember how Duncan was? He was attracted but
so angry. It was out of character. And me, I knew immediately
Molly was for me, even though I thought I would be alone the
rest of my life. You cannot decide. Out of character you might
say. If you feel the way you do, you need to find out if this is your
life partner."

She pondered his words for a moment, allowing the thought to sink in.

"So, I should go back and find out if he is for me."

"I believe that would be the wise thing. Don't you?"

"I think so. What about your future? Should I keep looking or believe in what the guardians have promised?"

"Yes, I think we should believe. Have they not been right so far? Believe me, when I say how hard it is for me to just wait and see what happens."

She sat there quiet. What would she do? He came and sat down next to her and took her hand.

"You are my sister and you have been protecting us since you were a child. I want to help you now while you have your doubts. Let me encourage you to find the happiness you deserve."

She squeezed his hand. Duncan loved her as did Hamish and now Alasdair was making it clear, he too loved her. Perhaps it was time for her to find love.

"I will go back. You are right, I must decide if he is for me. And I will do no more research. You have my word."

He put his arms around her shoulders, and she hugged him. "Thank you, Dair."

"You are more than welcome, little one."

* * *

THE NEXT FEW days Glenna enjoyed her own company. She walked around the estate even though the days were getting cooler. Some trees were losing their leaves, but the pines were ever green and magical. The scattering of rocks and grasses, the grey clouds and misty rain. This was what she loved about Scotland. Her mind was settled. Being in her home and time allowed her to think straight and decide what to do, along with Alasdair's help.

She would go back and spend time with Sinclair. She thought through all the times they had spoken and what she had already learned about him. One thing kept coming back into her thoughts. He had been alone all his life. He had no memory of any family. This disturbed her.

On one of her walks, Blake appeared.

"I have heard your question."

"You do appear at unusual times. What question in specific are you referring to?"

"His parents. Who were they?"

"Yes, I have been running the question through my mind." She stopped and looked at the fae who had become so familiar to her. She had no attraction to him. He created only curiosity in her thoughts.

"I cannot tell you. It is his question to ask of the fae."

"I totally agree. I would like to know. Perhaps one day he will ask the question and we will both know the answer."

"He is special. Not just to you but the fae."

"I agree with that observation also. I find him fascinating."

"Do you wish to know the future."

She sighed. "No. It is something I would like to find out for myself, if you don't mind." She looked at him and he returned her gaze with a smile. Then the teal blue light appeared, and he was gone.

"Bloody fae," she muttered and kept walking.

* * *

SHE WAS HOLDING her teacup in her hand and wishing she had one of those nice big mugs from the future. The teacups were fine but a big mug of tea, in the cooling weather, was so enticing. She looked forward to when she went back to the future.

She missed her morning cuppa with Molly. She understood

51

with her having gone to the future, her now husband Dair, had rightfully taken her place. But the 'girl' time, as Rachael called it, was so important to her. She missed her closeness to Molly. As if she sensed her thoughts, Molly came into the breakfast room.

"Am I disturbing your thoughts?"

"No, dear Molly. You were actually in them."

"I know. Accepting I am fae has revealed some of the magic I have been ignoring. I knew what you were thinking."

"That is such good news. Is it not?"

"Most definitely. I love magic. It is only the position of queen I do not wish to have." She came and sat down next to her.

"Thank you for all you have done to help me and Dair."

"It has been a pleasure."

"Now, tell me about the fae you are attracted to. It isn't Blake, is it?"

"No, Blake is a fae of mystery as is his 'nameless brother'."

"What is that all about? Why can't we know his name?"

"The guardians are secretive, but they do not have any malice in their nature. They love to protect their own kind, which includes you and me. They must have a reason for his name to be kept from us. It may reveal parts of the future they do not want to reveal just yet."

"That is as good a guess to their motives as anything I have tried to fathom." She laughed out loud.

Glenna smiled at her sister-in-law. "Are you happy?"

"Do not concern yourself with me, Glenna. I have never been happier. I miss those who I had in my previous life. But I have accepted they are gone. I have my Dair and my father. They are two wonderful gains."

"They are indeed." She paused and lowered her head, gazing into her teacup. "I have to go back."

"I know."

"I hope to return. I want to return."

"I know."

"I will miss you."

"I will miss you, too. But please work out what you want. You also deserve to be happy."

"Thank you, Molly. I will leave at sunset."

BACK IN 2020

*S*inclair was sitting and staring into space in front of him. Darn It was asleep on his lap. He had needed the cat close since Glenna had returned to her time. He could not believe she had left without saying a word to him. He had kept the note she had written saying she was going back and begging him not to continue the research. No explanation, just stop reading the diaries. That was hard for him. It was now his only link to her. He needed her in his life even if she didn't need him. He would remain alone it would seem. He may always be a Ghillies Dhu.

The door opened and closed behind him. He knew it was Duncan. They had their baby girl just before Molly went to the past. They wanted to move back to the cottage. He understood their need for privacy. For wanting to be a family. Clara was a beautiful little girl. And her nursery was lovely in the pale blue Rachael had picked for her bedroom walls. He had enjoyed the solitude of the cottage but knew he had to go back to the castle.

"I have not seen much of you, my friend."

"You have been preoccupied with Molly leaving and the arrival of your baby."

"That is true. But you have been even quieter than usual."

"Have I?" He looked at Duncan and gave a smile and knew his friend would see his sarcasm.

"I think we should talk."

"You need not worry about my blood mixing with yours. Your sister is gone. She has made up her mind."

"What the heck do you mean?"

"She has rejected me."

"Oh boy, you are thick. Rachael was right. You don't get it. Glenna was confused and scared. That is the reason she fled."

"So you say."

"I know my sister, and your admission in front of everyone scared her. That is why she went home. She was confused."

"Uhh…"

"I am right. I have never known her to be at a loss for words. And she was. She needed time to think."

Sinclair pulled the note from his pocket and handed it to his friend.

Duncan read it. "See? She would not ask you to stop reading the diaries unless she had a reason."

"And what reason could there be other than to show me my folly for falling for a fae who does not feel anything for me."

"I for one know Blake asked her to do no more research. He promised her no one would be greatly harmed or die."

"Blake asked her to stop the research. Not me. So why does she ask me to stop?"

"Perhaps she is afraid you will tell her if something terrible will happen?"

"That is not a good enough reason. She does not connect with me anymore."

"I believe you are wrong, my friend. I would be delighted if you became part of my family. I would not object to you."

"Yet, I am Ghillie Dhu."

"I know you. You are kind and sincere. You love history and

all that the fae offer. It would give me the greatest pleasure to welcome you."

He picked Darn It up and stood. Placing the cat on the warm spot he had just vacated; he watched the cat stand, stretch, and return to a ball position and go back to sleep.

"You are my friend. That will never change. As for your sister, I believe I will never see her again."

"That would be a pity. I think she will return."

He went to where his bag was waiting on the landing near the door. "I have packed. I have also cleaned the house. The fridge has been restocked and I have ordered cat food, which should arrive tomorrow."

Duncan reached for his wallet. "How much do I owe you?"

"Nothing, Duncan. It has been a pleasure to stay here. Go get your wife and daughter. I will see you later." He opened the front door to the cottage, smiled at his friend, picked up his bag and left.

* * *

"I TELL YOU HE IS HEARTBROKEN."

"I believe you. There is no smile, not even a hint of acknowledgement from him to anyone here in the castle. I am deeply concerned for him." Rachael placed her daughter on her shoulder to burp the babe who had just finished her evening feed.

"Then what are we to do?"

"Talk to him when you can. I do believe Glenna will come back. She too will want to know her true feelings. There was love in her eyes before she left. She just did not know it."

Duncan stood and took the babe from Rachael and continued to burp his baby girl.

Rachael rose and gave her body a stretch. "Let him keep reading the diaries. It will eventually tell him and us if she comes back. It may give him hope."

56

"Or he will become more morose."

"It is a chance we must take. We do not need to share anything with Glenna when she comes. But I believe Sinclair needs it before we lose him completely. I only wish we knew who he was related to. Why he believes he will be Ghillie Dhu for the rest of his life?"

Duncan leaned over and kissed his wife gently on the lips.

"You are very wise, my dear."

"Why thank you, sir. I will take that as a compliment."

* * *

Duncan did spend more time with Sinclair, and they continued reading the diaries. And he noticed a change in his friend. He became more hopeful.

"It says here Glenna returned to you for a short period of time. Alasdair gives no reason. Though he says to you. And I quote… 'You know how special our sister is. Her magic is such a special gift. I hope he will appreciate it.'"

"No name as to the 'he'."

"No. Perhaps later. I will keep reading."

He smiled at Sinclair and for the first time in many weeks he was hopeful things would become clearer soon.

TO THE FUTURE...

*I*t was dark when she appeared on the hill. But the moon was bright and high in the sky. She took a deep breath. The air was cool. It was cold but no snow lay on the ground. It must be late autumn or early winter. That would mean Molly had gone to the past.

She headed for the castle. She enjoyed the walk and was not surprised to see Sinclair heading toward her on the expanse out the front of the castle.

He took her into his arms and hugged her. She returned the hug, genuinely pleased to see him.

"I sensed you were here. I have missed you."

She pulled away from his hug and looked deep into his eyes. It was true, he had sensed her and genuinely missed her. There was some sort of connection to her. It was strange but encouraging. It seemed the connection between them still existed.

He took her hand and began the walk back to the castle.

"They predict snow tonight."

She looked to the sky and could see the clouds building up. Definitely snow ladened. In an hour or less the snow would fall, and the moon's light would disappear. She had arrived at a good time.

"How is Rachael? Has she had her babe."

"She has. Do you wish me to tell you, or would you rather wait to see for yourself?"

She laughed. "Please, Sinclair, I would be happy to hear you tell me."

"But don't you already know? After all, Molly has gone to the past with the knowledge."

"That is very true, but I want you to tell me as if I am hearing it for the first time."

"It is a beautiful girl. Clara. She is sweet like her mother. And I am watching her carefully to see if she shows any sign of magic."

"You may relax, Sinclair. If she has it, she will be five before we will know."

"Five, you say. I did not know that."

"It is just the way of things."

He led her through the front door and into the arms of Rachael who greeted her with enthusiasm. Duncan too was excited to see her as was the rest of her modern family.

"Come," said Laird Duncan, "and get warm. I will have food brought for you and a cuppa."

"Wonderful. And the biggest mug you have," she smiled at the butler as he went to get her food.

"You are looking well." Duncan added as he placed his arms around her. Sinclair had also not released her hand. He was hanging on to her.

"It has been a trying time. But the wedding went off without a problem."

"That is wonderful to hear. I am so happy my brother has found happiness."

"As am I," said Rachael.

"Molly was so regal as she told the guardians she had no

intentions of becoming a queen. You would have been so proud of her. And you have a daughter. I am so happy for you both."

"She is beautiful, and you will love her."

"I have no doubt about that. How could I not love my niece?"

* * *

As she ate, she listened to all the news from her family. They were able to do testing of everyone for Covid now and vaccinations would begin on December 8th, less than a week away. She was pleased to hear the news.

"So why have you returned?" her dear brother asked.

"That can wait." She looked at Sinclair and smiled. His face reddened slightly but he was grinning back at her. Okay, he was comfortable. "Tell me about Clara."

"No, we can do more talking tomorrow everyone. Let us leave Glenna to talk about the research with Sinclair." With Rachael's announcement everyone was up and out the door giving little time to say anything but good night.

"Rachael is such a forthright woman," Sinclair announced, still appearing rather red faced.

"That she is. The birth has not diminished her in any way. You would think she would be exhausted."

"Not in the slightest. They have moved back into the cottage and from what I have seen she is in her element."

"So, you kept reading the diaries?"

"Glenna, I really don't want to talk about diaries or research. I am sorry for the way I behaved when you were here last. I want you to know how much I have hated what I said and the way I said it."

"It is forgiven. And I need to ask you to forgive me for running away. Well, going home without talking to you. I am so embarrassed. I should have spoken to you and not just left you a note."

"Let us forget it and just be glad we are together again. Friends?"

"I am thinking we are both wanting to be more than just friends."

She leaned in and gently kissed his lips. He moved away for just a moment then placing his arms around, her returned the kiss and deepened it.

Her stomach was doing somersaults again. He did affect her in a way she had not experienced before.

"We must know more about each other. I feel I need to be near you. Since you left it is as if a part of me was missing. Please understand I do not feel like this normally. Things, events etc. go on around me but do not move me. But since you have entered my life, my life has changed. I want to know everything about you and your life. Does that make sense?"

She rested her head on his forehead. "It does make sense. You have moved me too. I do not get attracted to men in my time or other fae. Until I met you. I cannot explain it. We have a connection I have never had in my life before."

"So, what do we do now?" He stared into her eyes, and she could feel and sense him completely. No hidden thoughts. He was open and true to her.

"I imagine we explore what it is that draws us close."

He leaned in and kissed her again and she was sure the explosions raging in her body would consume her.

* * *

THEY SPOKE for hours about everything. Home in her past, the future, what she loved to do and what he loved.

If only this night would go on forever, and she could sit here listening to him talk.

At around three in the morning, he stood up and pulled her into a hug.

"We must sleep."

"Yes, I guess we must. We could…"

"No, my dearest Glenna. What the modern people of this generation do, I will not. I will only do what you are thinking when and if we marry. I will not treat you with disrespect."

"That is clear. But I was suggesting we could lay here on the couch and continue talking till we fall asleep. But thank you for your clarification."

She leaned up and kissed him on the lips, then turned and went out the door.

* * *

HE STOOD there feeling a little foolish. How could he have gotten her meaning so wrong? But he had every intention of bedding his red-headed beauty after they had married. But now he felt as if a ten-ton truck had just slammed into him. God, she confused him. What did she want from him? Did she want him? He walked to the door and turned out the light. He headed up the stairs to his room. Despite the confusion or misunderstanding, he knew what he would be dreaming about tonight.

GETTING TO KNOW YOU

The morning rain pattered on her window. She had left the curtains open last night as she wanted to wake when the light shone through. But it was a dull grey light. She did not care because the sun shone in her eyes. Thinking about Sinclair made her see the sunshine.

There was magic in him, and she adored him. And they would grow together and share the magic between them. She had no doubt they would be together forever. What an incredible revelation.

She got up and changed into her future jeans. She loved the trousers. They allowed her to move more freely than she could in the past. Women did not need to wear corsets either. Another great move to comfort. She did not like the bra that modern women wore. So, she left it off. She slipped a T-shirt on and pulled a sky-blue knitted jumper over that. It was cool now and she could almost feel the wind coming through the cold glass of her window.

She sat near the window and looked out at the modern world before her. A car was in the drive. The doctor. Cars are such a wonderful invention. She had not ridden in one as yet but was doubtful she wanted to try it out. She thought about where she wanted to live and in a pandemic was not what attracted her. Ideally, she wanted to go back to the world she knew. Would Sinclair go with her? Or would he want to stay here in the future?

So many questions. Too many. It would not be an easy question to ask. But for now, they were here, and she wanted to learn more about him.

She looked at the clock and saw that it was nine o'clock. She pulled on her socks and boots and headed downstairs in the hope of finding breakfast.

* * *

DUNCAN AND RACHAEL and baby Clara were at the table as was Sinclair. It was good that she could still see them. They ate their meals in the castle but spent their time in the cottage. The rest of the family must have had the meal and gone about their day.

She sat down next to Duncan, opposite Sinclair. His smile was broad, and Duncan must have noticed.

"I take it you two are an item."

She saw Sinclair's face reddened. Even his ears turned red.

"An item? What do you mean, brother dear?"

"That you are friends but in a special way."

Her face heated up and she was sure she too was blushing.

Sinclair responded.

"Yes, Duncan. We have an understanding."

She smiled.

"It's about time, that's all I can say." Rachael got up and handed the baby to Duncan and then leaned down and hugged her. She returned the hug, loving her friends matter of fact way. Rachael walked around to Sinclair and gave him a hug as well.

"Welcome to the family, Sinclair."

"Thank you, Rachael." She did not think his face could go any redder, but she was wrong.

"We will leave you to have breakfast together," her brother announced as he stood cradling his baby. Then he and Rachael left the room.

"I hope you did not mind my response."

She laughed. "Of course not. I believe we do have an understanding."

"Then we need to do a lot more talking. For one, where do I now stand with the fae? I do not want to be a Ghillies Dhu."

"It is not part of your nature?"

"Not anymore. I want to be with you, wherever that is."

She looked into his eyes and a smile grew on her face. He was for her, and she was glad.

"Perhaps we should go for a long walk after breakfast. I think you might want to ask yourself who you really are before you make any more decision."

* * *

SHE HAD HIT the nail hard. He had not thought about the question of his ancestry. But she was right. He needed to find out who his parents were and if he had any family left. But only so he could start a new life and family with his beautiful red-headed lady, Glenna.

They ate their breakfast in relative peace. She kept looking at him with concern in her eyes. She wanted him to deal with this question too. It was a way of moving forward. But it had to include Glenna. And he would tell the fae there would be nothing he would change. He just wanted to be with Glenna.

* * *

"I HOPE YOU DO NOT MIND…"

65

"Do not doubt what we have, Sinclair. We both feel we are to be together. Do we not?"

"We do. It moved so quickly. I do not want to doubt what we have."

The walk in the forest was the right thing to do. She could ask him questions without the fear of being overheard. It was cold this morning and they both had rugged up. One of her hands was gloved, and with the other, she held Sinclair's hand. Feeling flesh to flesh was reassuring. She was more relaxed when they were together.

"Let us find out what we can about your past. I believe you will be at peace when you know, and we can move forward and not doubt what we have found in each other."

"They are very wise words. You are wise, you know."

"Thank you. I do not feel I am wise but occasionally I come up with good ideas. Perhaps that makes me look wise." She held her head high and frowned.

He laughed and she did too.

"Do you think the guardians might know where I came from?"

"Yes. I wanted to know, and Blake said it was a question you needed to ask, not me."

"Have you seen Blake, then?"

"Yes, we had a number of conversations when I was home in the past."

"He asked you to stop your research."

"Yes, he did. Then I asked you to stop. Did you?"

"I did for a while. But I must admit I felt disconnected from you. Duncan suggested I begin again. So, I did."

"I understand. But I do not want to know anything else you may have discovered."

"I will not say anything to you. I continued for my benefit."

She stopped and looked into Sinclair's eyes.

"I want this. What we have is special. We are connected in a very special way."

"I agree, my love."

"My love. I like that."

He took her into his arms and kissed her.

Holding him and feeling his lips on hers, tasting his mouth and breathing in his scent was intoxicating. This was so what she wanted.

"Good morning."

"What the…"

"I apologize for the interruption. I sensed it may have been the right time to come and answer your questions, Sinclair."

He leaned his forehead on hers and chuckled.

"It is. You just took us by surprise."

"I stayed in my light for some time so you could notice it."

"No problem. My thoughts were elsewhere and your light did not penetrate my consciousness."

She gave his hand a squeeze.

"Would you like me to go?"

"No, I want you here," Sinclair said to her and then turned to Blake. "I would like some insight into my family history. If you would be happy to share."

"Very well. Your father was Prince Finbar of the Celeste family."

She saw his face pale.

"I am of royal blood?"

"Yes. You were another heir hidden from the queen."

"This is a joke."

"No. It is very true, and I am serious."

Sinclair let go of her hand and wiped his face with his hand. She could feel his sudden loss of identity and the fear that came with it.

"Sinclair?"

He did not respond to her plea.

"Sinclair?"

"I am all right. I just can't believe it."

"And his mother?" She looked at Blake, her hands firmly on her hips.

"She was fae also but a common fae."

"What happened to them?" Sinclair's head was lowered but she could feel his anger and confusion.

"Your mother died during childbirth. You were two years old. She and the babe died. Your father was devastated. He took you to stay with fae friends and he disappeared."

"Where did he go?"

"It is believed he went to the queen who killed him knowing he was a distant heir."

I AM LOST AND FORGOTTEN

He sat on the ground, unable to move. All the strength he might have had ten minutes ago escaped him now. Glenna came to sit next to him. He could see the fear in her eyes. She tried to smile but it was forced, and he could see that. This bond between them was never going to let him go. Not that he wanted it to. He felt like he had been kicked in the guts. He was royal. The queen… What did she know? Did she know of his ancestry? Was that why she came looking for him?

"The queen does not know who you are. The friends of your father looked after you until you were fifteen."

"I have no memory of these fae."

"No. Your memories were taken from you to protect you and you became Ghillies Dhu."

He felt ill. Nauseated, his stomach lurching. He buried his head in his hands, trying to stop his stomach from revolting. The fae had taken his memories and thrown them out like trash. How could they do that to him? His stomach ached and his head was spinning.

"We did this to protect you. We knew one day the queen would search for you, so we made you hard to find."

"Now you can read my mind and take away my memories. How do you expect me to trust you?"

Glenna remained speechless. She squeezed his hand to reassure him and herself, perhaps.

"We understand this is a shock to you."

"A shock? You have no idea. Everything I am, is a lie created by you, to protect me."

"We have protected you. Yes."

"But by taking away all I am. I have no memories even of those who protected me. I am having difficulties believing all of this."

Blake sat on the ground in front of him. He placed his hand on his shoulder.

"We did protect you. You were important to us. Your mother was my sister, Anissa."

Sinclair stared at the fae in front of him.

"How can that be? How could you be my uncle? You look the same age as me."

"I am fae in the fae world. Our life lasts longer than the fae who join the human world and we age very slowly."

"Explain. I do not understand."

"We placed you in the human world so you at least could live a life and not be found by the queen. You take on the life span of a human. Well, in part. You will live longer than a human but will have a shortened fae life. Glenna's mother became human so could be affected by human ways of dying."

"My mother died giving birth," Glenna spoke softly.

"Yes, she and your father had become human in an effort of staying away from the queen." He looked down at Sinclair. "But the loss of your mother drove your father mad. We believed he killed himself once he had found a home for you."

"I thought you said the queen killed him."

"Yes. But I think he allowed it, even wanted it, to take away the queen's chance to search for you. It is complicated. He told the queen his babe died with his wife and said nothing of your existence. So, he did kill himself you could say."

"This is all crazy. My parents are dead. And I have fae powers, but I am basically in human form."

"That is correct."

"What about me? How does my being with Sinclair affect things?"

"You are human but have fae powers."

"So, we are the same."

"I would say yes. Few humans have magical powers. You both have them because you are fae in a human world."

"I want to talk with Glenna, but I may have more questions for you."

"Just call my name and I will come."

Glenna placed her arms around Sinclair.

"Thank you for telling us, Blake."

Blake shone in the teal light and was gone.

"Are you alright?"

"As long as you stay with me, I am sure I will be fine."

"I am not going anywhere." She leaned in and kissed him on the cheek, then rested her head on his shoulder.

* * *

HER HEART WAS RACING, and confusion filled her thoughts. She could not imagine for a moment how her dear Sinclair was feeling. To be told you have no memories of your earlier life is bad enough. But to find out that a guardian, well more than one, are your uncles, was so very confusing. She could not believe how callously Blake told him. But then what else could he do? How do you break this kind of news to anyone?

"What are you thinking, Sinclair?"

71

"Confused, to say the least. I had no idea. I just accepted I had been Ghillies Dhu since I was a child. I guess that must be how the magic works."

"You are still you. Just that you are human with fae powers or fae living in a human world. Take your pick. It is good that you like humans. Who loves history and enjoys research. Who protected his friend and my brother. A man who is loyal and trustworthy."

"I guess but I am also a man who has little knowledge of his life till now."

"It still is you."

"Does my being royal, change your feelings for me?"

"No, why would it?"

"It might mean you are not safe with me around you."

"The same could be said for me being around Molly. But she is my friend, and I will remain close to her. She is family as are you. You are the man I have fallen in love with. I will be around you, too."

"Thank you, dear Glenna."

"No thanks are needed. I love you."

"And I you."

* * *

THEY WENT and explained things to Duncan and Rachael. It still seemed unreal and impossible to be true. She said a little prayer that Sinclair would come to terms with it. She gripped her hands tightly wanting her prayer to come true. He was blocking his thoughts to her again, but she understood why. He was trying to protect her as he sorted things out in his own mind. She could not be angry with him for wanting to protect her. But she also wanted to protect him.

"What other questions do you have?" She studied his brow as

it creased. He was thinking. She waited, giving him the time he needed.

"I wonder if I can get my memories back. I mean of my childhood with the family who protected me." Darn It stretched and resettled on Sinclair's lap. She watched as her love patted his ears and the cat purred loud enough to wake anyone who was nearby.

"We can ask Blake. And your uncles. They can tell you more about your mother and father."

"Yes. I think that is a wise idea. Sister, do you have questions?"

"What do you mean, Duncan?"

"I am very concerned for you. Sinclair, please don't misunderstand me. It is just that Glenna was young when she lost her mother. I was wondering," he said and looked at his sister, "do you have questions about our mother?"

"Dear Duncan."

"I agree, Glenna. In some ways we have had similar experiences. Do you?"

"No, my dear Sinclair and Duncan. For me it was not so hard. I missed my mother, but I had father and Hamish to help me through it."

"I feel so ashamed. I should have helped you more."

She came and placed her arms around her brother. "We all had lost our mother. And father especially found it difficult. But he spent a great deal of time telling me about her. Mother's kindness, her magic and all he could about the fae. It helped him to come to terms with his great loss. Hamish added all the stories mother had shared with him. I was very lucky. You and Alasdair did what you could, but we were all so sad at losing her."

"I want to know more about my mother and father. Also, my guardian uncles. I want to know where I stand in all this disturbance in the fae world. If I can help to bring peace..." He stared down at the cat and smiled.

Duncan came and stood before his friend.

"I want to help you through this…disturbance. I am so very sorry you have to go through this experience. What has happened to you is not fair. I cannot believe the fae could dismiss you so and…"

The teal light appeared, and Blake was there again.

Duncan swung around and grabbed Blake by the throat. "You had better tell us all right now, the whole story. Or I will drain the life from you."

"Duncan, let me go." Blake smiled at him, but the smile seemed strange as if he was worried Duncan just might hit him. Duncan eased off his grip.

"How could you do what you did…"

"We protected him. And might I remind you Duncan, this is Sinclair's questions to ask."

Duncan released his hold. "He is my friend. Just remember that."

"Believe me, Duncan. I am not likely to forget."

Blake sat on the coffee table in front of Sinclair. He reached out and patted the cat. Darn It moved his head and rubbed his hand with his whiskers and cheek, then went back to sleep.

"Cats are magical creatures. They trust very few humans or fae. But this cat knows I am telling the truth. I will answer all the questions you want."

"Can my memories be placed back?"

"Yes. We can see to it. Is that what you want?"

Sinclair looked at her. She nodded.

"Yes, I would like them back."

"Very well. Over the coming days they will be gently re-awakened in you. Just in small amounts. In around a week they will have all reappeared."

"My father. Tell me more of him."

"He was a prince and loved your mother greatly. He gave up his position in line to the throne to be in the human world, so he could raise a family away from the ties to the fae. He was tall and had red-brown hair. He had blue eyes. Your mother was beautiful, and she loved your father. Her hair was black as a raven. And her eyes were also dark. You look like her in coloring, but you are as tall as your father."

Blake was looking at his hands, deep in thought. "She was my sister and we loved her."

"Did you approve of the marriage?" Sinclair whispered.

"Yes. She was so very much in love."

Sinclair nodded.

Blake continued. "He worked in the government in Edinburgh. He loved being human. Your mother had no difficulties when you were born but two years later as she gave birth, to your brother…"

Sinclair began to pat Darn It's ears again. "A brother…"

"Unfortunately, he was born dead. Your mother hemorrhaged and they were unable to save her."

"We were all devastated at their loss. Your father fled for a few days, and you stayed with us. You could not understand what had happened, so we just played with you and tried to keep you distracted. When your father returned, he was somehow convinced the queen was behind the deaths. Nothing we said would change his mind. So, he started to look for clues. It was not true. No evidence was ever found."

"But the queen still killed him?"

"Yes. She could not stand his accusations and convinced the fae he had lost his mind."

"But before she did, he got you to safety with fae friends who took you on as their own. You will start to remember them."

"Gwen and Peter…"

"Yes. We watched over you. We are guardians and that is what we do. Eventually we helped you to become Ghillies Dhu. The rest you are aware of."

"Are you sure the queen was not behind my mother's death?"

"Yes. It has been examined carefully. She had no idea you had even been born. We wanted to keep it that way."

"Why Ghillies Dhu?"

"You loved being fae, so we left you a fae with your gifts but placed you in the human world. This could be managed. And it was. Until the queen came to see you. We thought she had found you out, but we soon learned it was merely a coincidence."

"Does she know now, who I am?"

"No, she has had no access to our information or asked any questions to concern us. We still believe you are safe."

Sinclair stopped and looked at his hands.

"Did my brother have a name?" he whispered.

"Maxen."

"Thank you."

The light came and went, and Blake was gone again.

WE WILL BE US

The next few days he took many walks. Some, Glenna was with him. Other times he asked to be alone. She never once complained or tried to change his mind. She allowed him what he wanted and needed to think things through. The memories of his time with Gwen and Peter were returning and a warmth of gratitude flowed through him. They were his family. They always told him the truth about his parents' deaths but just not the family lineage. They had been there for him through thick and thin. He knew he could count on them. He knew he would never be able to repay them for all their kindness and love.

His walks allowed his soul to heal. Walking in nature always provided him with peace. The colors, even in dull light fascinated him. The smell of the wet and damp mosses and rotting tree material. The sounds of scattering small animals in the under-growth. The added sound of birds at varying times of the day and the setting sun bringing the sounds of the evening animals to ear. He was fae, in human form, and in his element in nature. He did not want that to change.

"I noticed you have not been blocking your thoughts from me."

"Not anymore. I felt I needed to while I was sorting out all the memories. I hope you did not mind?"

"Of course not. I understood why. I am just glad to be able to hear you again."

He put his coat on as she did up the buttons on her coat. She had been very patient with him.

"I do not want to keep anything from you. I was reluctant to over burden you. From now on, I do not want secrets between us."

"They were not secrets. Inner thoughts need to be private. I am sure there will be times in the coming years when we will both block out our thoughts as we decide what we want to do."

"I suppose so." He took her hand as they went out the front door of the castle. They went down the stairs and headed for the forest. His favorite place.

"You know I love you."

"Oh yes. Those thoughts are clear and strong."

He smiled. It was true, he had no doubts about his love for Glenna. Nor of her for him.

"I want you to be able to see the truth in my mind whenever you look."

"And vice versa. I want the same."

"Have you given any more thought to our future?" She squeezed his hand.

"Yes. I would like to go to the past with you."

"Are you sure?"

"Yes. It seems the best place for both of us. I can do without the modern world. If I have books to read, and time in nature I am sure I will survive."

"I do not doubt that for even a moment. Then perhaps we should go back soon."

"If you like. But perhaps we should discuss it with the family. After all, the health of Scotland is in peril, at the moment."

"True. And we are not in a hurry."

"I would like for you to be married from your time."

"Are you asking me to marry you, Sinclair?"

He stopped and took her into his arms. "I guess I must be."

She laughed, reached up and kissed him.

* * *

"Well, I suggest we have an engagement party." Rachael was throwing her arms around them both.

"An engagement party? What is that?" Glenna shook her head.

"Very popular in these modern days, you could say." Rachael was very animated.

"But we are in lockdown. We can't do that." Sinclair was always practical, and he was right. Besides, she only knew the family, in this time.

"We can with the family as we are all here together."

She looked at Sinclair who was smiling. Perhaps they could?

"Very well. But let's make it a big affair."

"What do you mean, Sinclair?"

"Take lots of photos, dress up in formal wear. Lots of food and drink. A real party. If we must keep our distance, let's do it with style."

Rachael placed her hands on her hips. "Sinclair! You surprise me. You are the quietest person I know."

"That is true. But this is a special event."

"Okay. You have it. A big family party is what we need. Leave it to me."

"I had every intention of doing so. Now if you will excuse us, I have some more items I need to discuss with my fiancée."

"No problem. I will get back to you."

He took Glenna by the hand and led her into the library. She still loved to hold his hand and hoped she felt this way forever.

"You have made Rachael very happy. She loves to organize things."

"I know. It is her nature, you could say. Besides it will lift the spirits of all of us."

"She is right. You are normally the quiet one. Is this what you really want?"

"It is. It will be something special for us to remember with our future family. Now, let's sit down and talk about other things."

Glenna went to the sofa and sat down. Sinclair sat next to her.

"It is a strange question I want to ask."

"Intriguing. Please ask."

"I have no surname. Not one I want to use. Celeste is my past. Not what I want to take into my future."

"I understand. What were Gwen and Peter's surname?"

"They were Murrays, like you. But not related."

A chill went down her spine. But it was one of excitement, not fear.

"Why not keep their name? We can both be Murrays."

"Would it not feel strange to have your maiden name?"

"No. It is a name I am used to. But what do you want?"

"I would like to honor the family who raised me. But I asked the guardians to tell me what name my parents used before they died. It was Green."

"Green is the color of you. Your nature and love of the outdoors. I like Green."

"Well, what do you think of Murray-Green. It is the best of both."

"I like it. Green-Murray does not sound right but Murray-Green sounds perfect."

"Then, will you be happy to be called Glenna Murray-Green?"

"I will." She leaned over and gave him a kiss. "What else do you wish to discuss?"

He leaned his forehead on hers. "Reading my mind again, are you?"

"Yes. What else?"

"Children. Do you want children?"

She hesitated. She did not want to read his mind.

"Tell me honestly, please?"

"Yes, I do. I have loved my brothers and I want to enjoy sharing our children with them also. Growing up with them protecting me was a wonderful experience. Though I did not always see it like that." She lowered her head and her breath caught, waiting for his response.

"Wonderful. I was alone for so long. I want children. You are wise and I know you will help me when I fall short and am unsure what to do."

She leaned in and hugged this wonderful man. He wanted to have children as she did, and he glowed just thinking of the prospect.

"I would like to call our son, if we have one, Maxen."

She wanted to cry for his loss of his baby brother. "Of course. And perhaps Anissa for a girl, after your mum."

"Yes." He looked pensive. "I would like to do that."

She wanted to lighten his mood. "Perhaps Finbar we can give a miss."

"Perhaps. It does sound rather pompous and royal. I wonder what he called himself in the human world?"

Suddenly her thoughts were filled with Blake.

'Tell him Timothy'.

"Blake is telling me it was Timothy."

"Timothy Green. I like that. Please stay out of our thoughts, Blake." And he gave a chuckle.

LET'S HAVE A PARTY

The plans for the party seemed to be going well. Glenna was loving the reactions from Rachael as she got things done. Rachael was a whirlwind. Even in lockdown she was able to get her hands on so much for the party. She spent a great deal of time online ordering things. Packages were arriving daily, by the truck load.

"Glenna, come and see what has arrived."

"So much has arrived. I cannot imagine what could be so special that you need to show me."

Rachael had the box under her arm. She took Rachael with her other hand and led her into the library. "Just you wait and see. This will excite you."

"Okay, now you have my attention."

She closed the door and went to the desk and opened the box. Glenna came up behind her and could see a mass of blue material.

Rachael gently pulled out a dress and shook it out. Glenna was captivated. Delicate soft material fell to the floor. Dark blue as the night, with the moon shining on it. It shimmered as she moved the dress from side to side. What woman would not love a dress so beautiful, that it took her breath away.

"It's yours. Your engagement dress. Sinclair wanted you in formal wear and when I saw this, I knew it was for you. Put it on."

Glenna took off her jeans and threw her jumper to the floor. She stepped into the opening Rachael had made and pulled the dress up. She left her T-shirt on till she pulled the dress high enough to be able to take it off. Rachael came behind her, grabbed the T-shirt and did the zipper up on her dress.

"Wow, you look amazing."

She moved from side to side and the dress floated around her legs. The material was soft and light on her skin and shimmered as she moved. When she stood still it was as if stars were directing their light to her dress. It was glorious.

"We can't be at your wedding but at least we can celebrate your engagement. This is our gift to you, Duncan and I."

"Oh Rachael. This is too much."

"No Glenna. With what we have all been through it is not enough. But do me a favor."

"What is that?"

"Don't let Sinclair see it until the night. I want to make sure the photographer takes a picture of the look on his face."

Glenna looked down at the dress. It amazed her and she was sure Sinclair would be very impressed.

* * *

"I HAVE BEEN CHATTING with Blake again. They believe the queen will be taken into custody. Her magic will be taken from her. They also plan to keep her isolated in the future."

Sinclair took Glenna's hand and drew her to the seat under the great oak.

"Well, that is good news. Perhaps the unsettled state of the fae world will soon calm down."

"Perhaps. It is difficult to say. I know what still has to happen and I am concerned."

"Please Sinclair. Do not tell me. I do not want to know what will happen. It tore me apart having to go to the future and help Molly but not tell her anything. I do not want to know."

"I understand. I too want to allow the things to happen without affecting us. But I am not sure I can."

"Please, for my sake, try. After the party we will be heading back, assuming we are COVID free."

"You are right." He drew her closer to him and snuggled with her. It was very cool this morning, but he did like to be alone with her. When they returned to the past, they would not be alone until they married.

"Tomorrow night will be a great celebration. I hope you are happy."

"I am, Sinclair. No one could be happier than I."

"I think we are going to have years of happiness ahead of us."

They stayed under the oak tree and watched the movement of servants and the family in and out of the castle.

* * *

"LADIES AND GENTLEMEN, dear family. It gives me great pleasure to welcome you all here tonight. Please make sure you are wearing your masks and keep them on all evening. You can remove them to eat or while photos are taken. Now, let us welcome the man of the moment, my future brother-in-law, Sinclair Murray-Green."

Everyone clapped as Sinclair came into the dining room. He felt funny being in a tuxedo and being announced so formally. He had never worn such an outfit before. But he wanted things to be formal and Rachael had exceeded all expectations. He came and stood by Duncan.

"Now dear family, my sister, Glenna Murray."

Glenna drifted into the room. She was beautiful. The glorious blue dress sparkled as she came towards him. Her red hair was up, with flowers laced in her locks. She had make-up on, though she didn't need it. She was the most beautiful woman in the room and as far as he was concerned the whole world.

She took his hand as she reached him, and he was sure they only had eyes for each other. He leaned forward and gave her a gentle kiss on the lips. The room erupted in cheers, and he was brought back to earth.

"Cat got your tongue?" she asked.

"Yep. He had it for dinner."

She laughed and hugged him, and he laughed as he returned the hug.

* * *

GLENNA COULD SEE the stunned look on his face. He was impressed by the dress. Rachael said his mouth would drop open and it seemed she was right. She took his hand and joked with him to bring them down to earth. In this dress she imagined they were floating in the moon lit sky above. Everything felt right.

Duncan escorted them to their seats. They both put on their masks and then waited for Rachael's plans to begin. Everyone else went and sat in their allotted seats and so it began. The entrée was the first thing to be bought in.

Avocado Salad. One of her favorite things. She had never tasted an avocado before she came to the future. Seemed an appropriate start to the meal.

Everyone was chatting and laughing and having a wonderful time. They were all spread out so as not to be too close to each other. Except for her and Sinclair. The things they were expected to do. The doctor did not come, as he had COVID. In fact, many of the hospital staff had been falling victim to the terrible disease. This concerned her.

The main meal was veal roast. She had helped the cook to use the method her mother had to make the sauce for veal. In some small way she felt her mother and father were here. And soon she would be home with her family and marrying the man she loves.

Duncan stood.

"It is my turn to speak. I want to say how excited I am that my little sister will get married. Although we will not be able to attend the wedding, I am delighted, as is Rachael, especially as we can share this special evening with them."

Glenna felt lightheaded. She had dreamed one day this very experience might happen. Now, it was. But something did not feel right. She did not know what it was. She pushed the feeling down to the pit of her stomach. That is when the teal light again appeared.

Duncan's fist hit the table. "You can't leave us alone, even when you were not invited? What the hell do you want?"

"We are sorry for the interruption."

Duncan sat down. "I bet."

"We need to speak with Glenna and Sinclair."

Sinclair stood. "Go to the library, uncle. We will meet you there shortly."

Rachael came over to Glenna. "You think the fae who can travel in time would pick a better moment."

Duncan's fist again hit the table.

Sinclair turned to him. "Keep going, Duncan. Finish your speech. They can wait."

Duncan stood and lifted his glass. "Let us hope the life Glenna and Sinclair have from here on is less complicated than what they have been going through. Lift your glasses to Glenna and Sinclair."

"Glenna and Sinclair." Echoed the voices of all who were present.

Many came over and congratulated them and after a short time, Sinclair took Glenna by the hand. "Let us get this over and done with. We will listen to what they have to say and send them on their way."

"Very well."

They made their way to the library.

THIS HAD BETTER BE A JOKE

The walk to the library was without further conversation. Sinclair was not happy and if she could describe how he felt she would say steam was coming out of every orifice in his head. They entered the library.

"Do you really think popping in when we are having a celebration is appropriate, uncle?" His hands were placed firmly on his hips.

"We are your family too, and you chose to ignore us."

Glenna was pacing back and worth. "This is for my future family as they will not be able to attend our wedding. You would have been invited to the wedding."

"We have not come to complain about invitations. We have a proposition for you." Blake straightened himself and placed his hands behind his back.

"Then get on with it." Sinclair stood there tall and determined with his hands behind his back. Seeing the men mirroring their stance sent a chill down her spine. He had become a force to be reckoned with since his memories had returned. He was still the gentle man she had always known, but was more determined.

"We know who the new queen will be, but she is yet to be born."

"So? What is that to us?"

"We need an interim queen till the time is right."

Everyone's eyes shifted to her.

"No, no, no, no."

"It will only be for a short time, your highness." Blake bowed.

"Do not highness me. You dare place this burden on me? I am of no royal blood."

"But your betrothed is."

"Excuse me? You have hidden me from sight and now you want us to be placed in the firing line for the queen to target us? I agree this is nuts."

"It is complicated. But one of your descendants will become queen. I cannot say who or when exactly it will be. But we need an interim queen."

"I won't do it."

"How will our 'filling in' be helpful, Blake? Especially, as you will not explain what is going on."

But Glenna didn't give Blake the chance to answer. "Who cares? I will not put myself or you in the situation, Sinclair."

"It is my decision to make, who I help. I do want to help if I can. I know more now about my family than I did."

"You go ahead and help them. I have no intention of doing so. They have caused chaos in the fae world. And in our world."

Sinclair turned and faced her. "That is not fair. The queen is the one who has disturbed the fae world."

"Only in part. These guardians have been running around chasing us from one time period to another, to achieve what they want."

"Glenna, that is not right." He placed his hand on her shoulder.

She shook him off. "Isn't it? Well, my dear, you help them all you want. I am going home. I refuse to do what they want."

"But the party?"

"What are we celebrating?" She threw her hands into the air. "It is obvious to me you wish to help them, and I do not. That places us at odds with each other, does it not?"

She turned to Blake. "Thank you for ruining our party and engagement. I will return to my time and you two can sort out what you want to do."

"But Glenna, what about us?"

"Us? I do not believe there is an us. Not anymore."

Tears were brimming in her eyes as she turned and fled.

* * *

He wanted to run after her, but he knew she was mad and needed time to calm down. But he had to agree their world had turned upside down.

"Blake, you are fae guardian. You travel in time regularly."

"Yes. What point are you trying to make?"

"Can you not go to the future and bring your queen to this time or whatever time you get rid of the other queen? Why place us in danger? We have done everything you wanted, haven't we?"

"It has not been done before."

"But it is possible?"

"Yes, it is."

"Then do it and end this saga. Now if you will excuse me, I need to find Glenna."

"She has gone home."

"I know. I will go and talk to her."

"No, I mean back to the past."

"Already?"

"Yes, she went straight to the hill from here. By the time you reach the hill she will be gone."

"You really do not understand what you have done."

"She needed to go home to balance the timelines."

90

"Blake, the timelines have been mangled for some time. Look at what you have interfered with. Molly. Now she lives in the past. Duncan, he lives in the future. Me. Where the hell do I belong? And poor Glenna has tried to make head and tail of it all since it started. No wonder she ran home. I see she is the only one who could see the truth."

"We cannot predict what will happen. It is decided by each individual."

"Is it? With your popping in and out of times and places it would appear to me that you are trying to dictate what will happen."

Blake stared at him.

"That has not been our intention."

"It may not have been. But it has been the result. Go back to the fae kingdom and get your queen in place. Glenna is right. This has gone on long enough. And leave us alone."

Blake bowed and his teal light took him home or wherever he needed to go.

Sinclair stood there for a moment. Glenna had gone back to the past. It was time for him to impress her, on her fortitude and determination, to marry the woman he loved. He headed back to the party to prepare what needed to be done.

RETURN TO DECEMBER 1823

She was in the house at Charlotte Square. This was strange. The fae brought her to where Molly and Alasdair were rather than to the fairy Hill near the castle. She wanted to be with them not the castle. She could hear voices coming from the sitting room. Voices she recognized. She stood outside the door and listened.

"Da, I don't want you to kill anyone. And I don't want you to get damaged either. I just want this to go away."

It warmed her heart to hear how Molly had accepted Sen as her father. She had fitted into her new life here in the past so easily. Yet, her strength was what amazed her more than anything else.

She heard Molly speak again.

"Dair, I love you and have no intention of going anywhere. This is what I want. You. And the baby. And Da."

This seemed the perfect time to let them know she was home.

"What about me? Do I come into this equation?"

Molly jumped up and ran to her. She threw her arms around her and hugged her. Alasdair came over and wrapped his arms around them both.

"Welcome home, sister."

Glenna pulled herself out of the hug and examined Molly's arm. She still found it difficult to believe the queen had attacked her and Sen. Then she looked at the paling face of Sen.

"I am sorry."

Alasdair took her into his arms. "Tis not your fault, Glenna. You are not to blame."

Her face heated up. She blamed herself for what had happened to them. She kept her head down and avoided eye contact If only she could make it right.

"Maybe. But I can be angry, can I not?"

"Of course, you can, Glenna. But we just want the whole thing to stop."

She hugged him back.

"Blake has promised me it will end and soon." She didn't want to tell them she had run from the future again. That she had been offered the chance to be the queen and she had thrown it back at them. She just hoped her white lie would be true in the long run.

"You have been talking to Blake?" Molly asked.

"Yes," she replied. "He is in the future, trying to sort things out." She wanted to cry knowing that her beloved Sinclair would rather help the guardians than her. "I told him I was coming home and here I am."

Molly wrapped her arms around her again. "And here you are. Tell us what you have been doing."

"Not now. I want a bath and a change of clothes. Please be patient, I will tell you all. Just not right now."

Molly looked deep into her eyes. Glenna could see her understanding her thoughts. Her magic was stronger. She whispered in her mind 'I will tell all later.' Molly nodded her understanding, and she nodded back at Molly and turned and left the room.

* * *

IN HER BEDROOM, she sat on her bed. The maid came in and prepared the floor with a blanket, ready for the bath. It came in with the servants a few minutes later. Soon the bath was filled, and she was left alone.

She took off her beautiful dress and placed it on the bed. She was glad she had not changed before leaving the future. She wanted to keep the dress as a reminder to her of what could have been. All she did was grab her bag that she had prepacked ready for a quick escape. Then she wept. Tears poured from her eyes. Everything had gone wrong. Why did she lose her temper? Sinclair must hate her, now she had fled to the past again. But she could not have stayed and been a party to the ridiculous idea of her being queen.

She slipped into the water and allowed its heat to seep into her soul.

Why had she gotten so angry? Justice kept repeating itself in her mind. Yes, she was a justice seeker. Someone who wanted to help everyone to get what they deserved. She had given her life to her brothers to protect them from the fae, and to help them find the loves of their lives. But she had sacrificed her own happiness to do the right thing. Surely the fae, and the guardians especially, could make this right without turning her into the queen? Something she was not.

So much had happened to them all. And the fae was behind so much of what they were going through. Could she forgive herself for ever getting involved in their mischief? She had to think about that.

She got out of the bath and dressed for bed. It had been a long day spent in two different times. She needed to sleep.

* * *

GLENNA SPENT the next day adjusting to being home in her own time. It had eased her mind to see Molly glowing with life despite

94

the attack by the queen. Knowing that a baby was on the way added to the joy she could see. What the queen had done angered her so very much. She wanted to call Blake and thought better of it. The less she saw of him now, the better she would be.

She tried to distract herself by reading. That worked for a few minutes but soon her thoughts were back to the fae and what they were up to.

Molly sat with her and told her what she remembered about the attack. Although it angered her a great deal, it seemed to help Molly, helping her come to terms with what happened.

That evening they had dinner together. Hamish came and stayed in the Charlotte Square house as well. All the family together. Well, no Duncan or Rachael but she knew they were in the right place.

"I brought back some Ibuprofen for you. Not a great deal but surely enough for you and Sen to use at the moment. It should help you feel better."

"Thank you, Glenna dear. It will be used for Da. He needs it more than I."

Glenna studied her features. Molly was flushed and tired. The last few months had been obviously more stressful than she had given thought to. This only added to her feelings of guilt.

"A babe is such a blessing," she added.

And Molly's demeanor changed. Joy filled her eyes and her smile widened. This was the real joy. A baby was to be a great blessing for them all.

* * *

GLENNA HAD PREPARED a list of things for Alasdair to have made for the baby. This had excited her brother.

"It is called a change table. Rachael had one and it was very useful."

She handed the list and the drawings to her brother.

"I will have Mr. Trotter arrange to build them and all items will match. It is a small thing, but I want Molly to have the best of what we can give to her."

"I know, brother. I am sure the worst is over, and things can only get better from here."

"I am sure. Tomorrow, spend the day with her and Hamish and I will arrange for the furniture to be made and sent to Castle Buin as soon as it is possible."

"I will, brother."

"Do you plan to tell me what you have gone through in the future?"

"Eventually. But some of it still upsets me, Dair. I am not ready."

"Very well. But you are sad. I can see that much. Do not leave it long before you talk with one of us."

"Yes, brother. I will. I promise."

2 020

"All I can say is if a guardian shows up here again, I will knock him out before he has a chance to do any more damage."

Sinclair laughed. He had to agree with Duncan. Hitting Blake square in the face felt like the thing he wanted to do.

"I directed him to get the future queen and bring her to a point in time where she can take control. I see why Glenna was so angry. The fae can move in time and they had not even thought of doing that very thing."

"The last thing Glenna would want to be is queen. They must have known her thoughts," Rachael added.

"Agreed. But I did not see or understand how it was affecting her. Not straight away. I think I would have run away too."

"She did not run away. She went home. She had enough of the guardians. Do not hold her going home, against her. She loves you. She was just so angry, and I don't blame her for that."

"Nor do I. I hope she knows I will come to her."

"I think I know Glenna well enough now. She will be kicking herself that she fled. But she will accept you with open arms when you go back."

Duncan placed his hand on his shoulder. "When do you plan to go?"

"Ahh. Thanks to your suggestion to continue to read the diaries, I know exactly when I will go." He pulled the diary from his jacket and handed it to Duncan.

"Just read the pages from the first bookmark to the second bookmark. I know I am doing the right thing. All will be well."

Duncan was scanning the diary.

"Are you still getting married?" he asked.

"As far as I am concerned, yes. But ultimately it is Glenna's decision. I did not keep reading once I found that entry. I want us to go on without history telling us. If you know what I mean. I will tell her how much I love and want to be with her, but it is up to her. Nothing is written in stone. Not even the diaries."

"Just say what you just said when you see her, and all will go well."

Rachael hugged him.

"Ahh, I see. Do what has been described here and you will have won her heart forever. Heaven help the guardians. I would not want to be in their shoes when Glenna is around. They will regret having upset her."

Rachael took the diary from her husband's hand and began to read it.

"I hope so. I know Glenna wants to help her family and she has done more than most. She wants all of you to be happy."

"But we want the same for her. She deserves it."

"Oh my. Sinclair, this is amazing. You have to go and win her heart like this."

"That is my intention. Will you help me prepare to do this?"

"Most definitely."

"You can count on us." Rachael was hugging him again.

Molly had the stitches removed from her arm yesterday and was ready to go home. Though Sen was still not well, Glenna was glad they had agreed to be home by Christmas. Although Molly was clear to point out, next year Christmas would be a much bigger event than what they were used to.

Glenna was happy to be heading home. She had metaphorically kicked herself many times since she got to Edinburgh. She longed for Sinclair to come back to the past to find her. Would he understand why she had left? She asked herself these things over and over. Deep down she knew the love they had for each other would bring them back to a place of understanding. But she had promised not to run away again. Although she was escaping the guardians not him. Sinclair might have thought she was running from him.

They stopped for the night at the inn in Perth. She did all she could to help Sen to eat and have a good night's sleep. Molly was comfortable and was just glad to be going home. At least the weather was fine. If it was raining the roads would soon turn to mud.

The next day they travelled to Pitlochry. The weather was still good, and she was glad to see the countryside of Scotland she loved in the time she loved. The inn was warm and welcoming when they arrived.

The next morning the rain had started and made the going tough. The rain was light but so cold. It added to all of their discomfort. After more hours than she wanted to remember they made it to Dalwhinnee. They were close to home now and her feelings of foreboding were weakening. The inn keeper was well known to them and made them welcome. All of them had an early night. They were tired of travelling and wanted to be home.

The rain persisted on the fourth day. Alasdair wanted to continue before the weather got worse. She was glad the snow had not started. It would have been harder to get home then. The day went slowly but they made it to the final stop before they reached home. Cromdale, just after Aviemore. It was very cold. It was much higher in altitude than the other stops and so close to the Cairngorms. And about an hour before they arrived it began to snow. It was light but could make the last part of the trip longer and more difficult.

John Boag, the inn keeper came out to greet them as the carriage pulled up.

"Welcome, friends. Please come in and make yourself warm."

Alasdair jumped out of the carriage and greeted John with a hug. The families of Boag and Murray had been close friends for many years. Arriving here, they knew they would be home at Buin Castle by luncheon time tomorrow. Unless a snowstorm hits tonight.

"Welcome Lady Molly and dear Glenna. We will have a beautiful meal for you. Go to the sitting room when you are ready. And your usual rooms upstairs are ready for you now."

"Thank you, John. It is so nice to be near home."

Glenna helped Sen and Molly out of the carriage. Sen decided to have a meal in his room and get to bed early. She helped him with his luggage and then went to her room to freshen up.

* * *

GLENNA MADE HER WAY DOWNSTAIRS. She was tired and hungry and thought she would get to bed early. She entered the private dining room they always used. Alasdair and Molly were already there and talking to John. Food was laid out on the table. Soup and freshly baked bread. There was dried fruits and cheese as well as hot tea.

She sat down with a bigger sigh escaping her lips than she had intended.

"Thank God we will be home tomorrow." Molly looked at her with pity in her eyes.

John poured her a cup of tea and she sat back in her chair and sighed again.

"Enjoy your meal, Miss Glenna. If there is anything more you want, just ring the bell."

John turned and left the room.

"Now sister dear, it is just the three of us. Please tell us what has happened in the future and why you returned when you did."

"I am sorry, Dair. It has been a chaotic time for all of you and I did not want to burden you with my concerns."

"Glenna dear, you are my sister. I can tell you have suffered, by coming home when you did. You have been sad, melancholy if you like. Just tell us what it is that brought you home."

It was an invitation to open the flood gates. And she did. She shared everything. From when she returned the last time to coming suddenly home to Edinburgh days ago. She told them of her love for Sinclair and her hope he would forgive her for coming home. She shared her anger with the guardians and them wanting her to be queen. It all flowed out and she finally let out a sigh of release that surprised even her.

"If they dare show themselves again…" Alasdair clenched his fists.

"I doubt they will come anywhere near me again. Duncan wanted to throttle them, too."

"We are your brothers. Did you think we would stand idly by?"

She laughed. "I never thought about that."

"I cannot believe the guardians would put you in a situation like that. They really are nuts." Molly was shaking her head.

"I never thought nuts would have such a big meaning in my life." They all laughed.

Glenna was eating all the beautiful food as they chatted. It was so good she could finally talk with her family about all that had been going on.

"Why did you waited to tell us all that had been going on?" Molly asked.

"You had been through so much. To be wounded by the queen and nearly lose your father. I could not burden you with my story."

Molly grabbed her hand, and she could feel the love from Molly pulsating into her fingers. "We are family, dear Glenna."

Months of emotional trauma overflowed. Glenna wept as she had never wept before. She knew the truth. They were all family. Now all she needed was her Sinclair and all would be well.

Reading her mind, Molly added, "He will come to you. He loves you. How could he not come? Before you know it, he will be here. Well, at least he will come to you wherever we are."

"Molly, you are wonderful. Thank you. I have hope."

"Would you go back to him?" her brother asked.

"No. I doubt the guardians would allow me to travel again to the future. Besides, this is my home. Scotland, in this time. I hope Sinclair will understand and come to me."

"He would be a fool if he did not." That was all her brother could add. And he was right. But Sinclair was no fool. He would come. She had to believe that, over everything else.

* * *

THE NEXT MORNING a light drift of snow lay on the ground. If they took their time, they would make it home today. Their luggage cart left early and after a beautiful breakfast of dried fruit, bread and honey they were on their way home.

The atmosphere in the carriage was lighter. Even Sen was feeling much better and looked forward to getting home. But the day dragged on. And at last, the castle came into view. She sighed a breath of relief. She was home at long last.

HOME AT LAST

olly was tired and after being greeted by the servants and congratulated on her condition, she went upstairs to have a bath and go to bed. Glenna made sure everyone's luggage had been sent to the right rooms and made sure that Sen had been set up in a family room near Molly. She knew Molly would want him close so she could keep an eye on him.

Some hours later Glenna came down for dinner and was greeted by her brother. He was concerned for Molly. He explained she was extremely unsettled.

"You have to see it from her point of view, Dair. She has been attacked by a stranger, as has her father. Though Sen knows what the queen looks like, Molly does not remember her attacker. It happened so quickly. Perhaps I should introduce Sen to the new staff and see what the reaction is."

"Perhaps it is a wise thing to do. Molly seems to be on tenterhooks."

"I think it is understandable. If it gives her peace, I will do whatever she wants."

"As will I. I do not like seeing her like this. She is growing as the babe gets bigger. And I know she does not want to do anything that might bring risk to the bairn."

"I know what Rachael was like when she was pregnant."

"That's right you do. Is Molly behaving in a similar way?"

"The situation is very different, but tears are the most common thing. Either of them can start crying at the drop of a hat. Rachael said it was hormones. Something in the blood that changes when you are expecting a child."

"Then we just need to watch her and do whatever makes her comfortable. I do not want her to be suspicious of the staff who love her."

"I think you are right. The staff love her and any new staff I will deal with. Just stay close to Molly."

"I will, Glenna. Thank you."

He finished his wine and stood and gave her a kiss on her forehead. "I am glad you are home."

Glenna walked through the house, taking in all the familiar sights and smells. She smiled as she remembered all the happy times she had spent here. This was her home. This was where she belonged. Now she really prayed that Sinclair could hear her thoughts. She was home but wanted him here too.

After her brother left, she asked the butler to fetch Mrs. Gillies and Mrs. Boyce. She wanted to do everything she could to help Molly and comfort her.

She finished the last of her food on her plate as the ladies entered.

"Please sit down, ladies. I need your help."

They ladies looked at each other, confusion written on their faces and sat down opposite Glenna.

"As you are aware, Molly has been through a great deal these past months. She is with child and is still recovering from the attack on her person. We need to look after her and protect her."

"Of course, mistress. We will do anything to help Mistress Molly."

"Thank you, Mrs. Boyce."

"All the staff adore her, mistress," Mrs. Gillies added.

"Well, that might not be the case. We have some new staff members. I would ask that you get Sen to meet all the new staff. He knows the face of the one who attacked them. Let him make sure they are not enemies."

"Of course, mistress. What else can we do?" asked Mrs. Gillies.

"We want her to rest but also keep her occupied. Sit with her and help her to plan Hogmanay. But also plan a special dinner for Christmas day. Christmas means a lot to her. Find out what she wants, and do it if you can."

"We will, mistress. You can trust us to help her."

"I thank you, ladies. I know you love her and Master Alasdair. We want them to be relaxed and happy in their own home."

Both ladies stood. "We will keep you posted, mistress."

"That will be wonderful, ladies. And Mrs. Boyce, are you able to get for me an empty journal that I could use, please?"

"Certainly, mistress. I will have it sent to your room."

The ladies departed and the footmen and maids came in and cleared the table. Her mother's beautiful table. Given to her by her father. She had seen it here in the past and in the future. It was a valuable family cornerstone. One that would follow the family for centuries to come. It had not escaped her to see the importance of what she had been through in her own life in the past few months. Now, she just needed Sinclair to return and all would be right in the world.

* * *

GLENNA ENTERED HER BEDROOM. The maid had made her a fire. A small scotch whisky was on a table next to her chair before the fire. She closed the door and saw that Mrs. Boyce had left a journal on her bed.

Picking it up she walked to the table and placed it on it. Then she went to the window and pulled the curtain aside and watched the snow falling. Home. This was what she wanted. To be in her home. Although it was her brother's inherited right, this was where she felt at home. The modern world, she was happy to leave ahead of her. But she missed one very important thing. Her Sinclair. She had fallen in love with a fae who loved humans so much that he had chosen to live with them. Could she ever hope to see him again?

Over the last few days, she had come up with a plan. She needed to let him know that she still loved him. She could not go back into the future. She doubted the guardians would allow her. She would keep a short journal. Where she could tell him how she felt. One day he would read it. She would place it with her brother's diaries in the library.

Having made up her mind she had asked for the journal from Mrs. Boyce and as she had hoped it was the same kind of book her brother used to write his diary to Duncan.

So, she would write as much as she could between now and Hogmanay. It seemed Hogmanay was the right time to place the diary into the library. Before a new year could start, she would explain to him her love, her concerns, her temper which often allowed her to get into trouble. And she knew where to place it knowing he would one day read it and in hope she would wait to see if he came to her.

If he did not, then she knew he was not her soul mate. That the fae would need to allow her to take a different path. She closed the curtain and went to her bedside table. She picked up the pencil she always kept by her bed and went and sat in the seat by the fire. Picking up the journal, she opened to the first page and began to write...

My dear Sinclair.

CHRISTMAS DINNER

$\mathcal{M}$olly was still on tenterhooks. She spent most of her time in the kitchen with Mrs. Gillies or in her room with either her father, Sen, or Alasdair. Occasionally, Glenna would spend time with her. It was Christmas day and Molly was feeling particularly glum.

"I wanted to have a real Christmas. One like I use to have with my mum and sister."

"I am sure it can wait till next year. You had no time to prepare for this year. But you do have time to prepare Hogmanay."

"I know. Mrs. Gillies is sharing all the traditions of the family and of Scotland in relation to the celebration. And I am excited by it. It is still a week away. And today is Christmas."

"Well, I am happy to tell you we have prepared a lovely Christmas dinner for this evening."

"Have you? Oh, that will be wonderful. I am sorry to be moaning about it."

"Do not apologize for the way you feel, Molly. I want to celebrate your kind of Christmas too. But your health and that of the baby is far more important. And you will be well rested by

Hogmanay. So, tonight is just a taste of what it will be like when you can organize properly next year."

"Thank you, Glenna. You are so very thoughtful."

"You are very welcome, my dear sister. For that is what you truly are."

* * *

THAT NIGHT EVERYONE in the family who were in the castle got together for Christmas dinner.

Even Sen seemed to be in the mood to do a bit of celebrating.

The dinner was a crowning success. Mrs. Gillies had gotten many ideas from Sen, of what Christmas was like in the future. A large piece of roast beef, with gravy and roasted vegetables was the main course. And fruit cake and brandy custard were for dessert. He kept referring to it as pudding. There was talk of next Christmas and lots of laughter.

"And next year we will have my grandchild to fuss over." Sen then stood up and went to the sideboard. Gifts were wrapped in plain brown paper waiting for him to give them out. He had carefully added a trig off a pine tree to each package.

"My dearest Molly, I know how badly you wanted Christmas so I arranged this time with Glenna so we could spoil you just a little bit."

"Oh Da, and Glenna. Thank you for thinking of me."

"Now to the gifts," Sen continued.

He picked up a small square package and handed it to his daughter. Molly took it, smiling the whole time at her Da.

Glenna noticed a small tear slide down her face.

Molly opened the small package. It was a ring. But a very special ring. It had a yellowish stone in it.

"It is a cairngorm stone. Very Scottish and very much you. I give it to you, my dearest daughter."

She took it from the box and placed it on her middle finger on her right hand. It fitted perfectly.

"It is beautiful, Da. Thank you. I am sorry I have no gift for you."

"On the contrary my dear, you are the greatest gift I have ever received."

"I agree, Sen. Thank you," said Alasdair.

Alasdair and Molly were so perfect together. She could see the love in their eyes, and it made her heart soar. They were so happy together. Molly had once lost so much but she had now gained more than she could have ever imagined.

Sen then handed a long package to his son in law. Alasdair took the gift and unwrapped it. It was a riding crop.

"I made it with my own hands."

"Thank you, Sen. It is beautifully made."

And it was. Sen had outdone himself. He reached for another gift which could easily be a book wrapped in brown paper. He handed it to her.

"Sen. This is unexpected. I have no gift for you."

"You need not give me a gift. Your acceptance of me into the family is all I need."

Glenna jumped up and hugged the dear man. He had certainly become a family member and she cared for him a great deal. She came back to her seat and unwrapped her gift. It was a leather-bound note book. He had placed the leather on a journal and carved her initial into it. 'G'.

"I noticed you writing in a journal the other day and I thought you might like a special one."

"It is very special, Sen. I thank you with all my heart."

"You are more than welcome."

"Next year Da, we will have Christmas and it will be special. But not as special as you have made today."

Alasdair stood and got the whisky from the sideboard and the butler placed glasses on the dining table in front of him. Dair poured whisky into each glass and handed one to each of the family.

"I propose a toast. To Sen, for his magical Christmas. To my darling wife, for our precious package yet to come. To my sister, who has come home. I salute you."

And everyone held their glasses in the air and said, "Slainte."

GETTING READY FOR HOGMANAY

The coming days were full of joy and laughter. One of the things Glenna loved about Hogmanay was the traditional cleaning of the castle. Everyone joined in and Molly was delighted to learn of all the traditions. She helped to direct Mrs. Boyce with what to clean and get ready for the day. Everything was scrubbed and polished. She wrote all about it in the journal she was planning to leave for Sinclair.

Glenna was sitting in a chair by her window allowing the light to stream through the window. The windowpanes were frosted over, and she could see her breath in the air. She shivered as she pulled her robe tighter around her. The fire was lit and warmed the room well, but the cold seemed to seep in through the cracks around the windows. She looked out the window at the snow-covered ground. It was a beautiful sight, but it also made her shiver.

She turned back to her journal and wrote about the cleaning and how Molly had taken to it. It put a smile on her face telling Sinclair about her days and her reactions to being home. Glenna had spoken to her this morning about any debts that were owed and how all would be paid off before the day. Even the villagers and tenants were doing the same. There was a lightness in everyone's steps. For the last few years there had been little to bring joy to the estate but now everyone seemed to be in high spirits.

She also shared with Sinclair about the arrival of a stranger on the stroke of midnight on Hogmanay. And that the stranger had to have black hair. Why? She could imagine him asking. They believe it was so significant that the visitor was not a Viking who had come to destroy the village or house. She wrote:

I love the sense of peace and tranquility the stranger would bring to the evening. And the gifts he would bring with him in a basket. Shortbread. So very Scottish. A lump of coal and a log of wood for the fires that would soon be lit. You see, we clean out all the fireplaces and remove the ash, which is buried in a hole, signifying the death of the old year. So, coal and wood can be used to light the new fires in the hearths for the new year. A bottle of whisky is added to the basket, also very Scottish, as is bread and salt for seasoning and life. It is such a memorable occasion. Mrs. Boyce has a relative coming who has black hair, so I imagine we will have our stranger. One day, I hope you will be here to see it all happen.

Glenna stopped writing and looked out the window. There she saw Alasdair and Molly walking in the snow. The sun was shining despite the cold weather, but the clouds were building, and she sensed the doom of a storm on the horizon. After the joy she had been writing about this morning, she shouldn't be thinking about doom and storms.

* * *

THE NEXT DAY a thick blanket of snow lay everywhere. It was so beautiful. Glenna wrote of it in her journal to Sinclair. Later that morning she had tea with Sen.

"I told Molly this morning, I have checked all the new staff. There are no fae, nor my mother in disguise amongst them."

"That is so good to know. I do hope the knowledge will help her to relax and enjoy the season."

"She says she is feeling much better. As am I. It was a difficult time for the both of us, but we seem to be healing."

"How does your shoulder feel?"

"I must admit it is taking me a while to recover. I am not sure I will ever be the same again."

"You still have a lot of healing to do. There is no need for you to be in a hurry. What is the rush?"

"I have a job to do. I need to manage the estate."

"But you're Molly's da. You do not need to continue working."

"It is nice to think I do not have to continue but it is my job."

"Sen, take the time to recover. It is winter and we are all taking the time to begin a new year. Think about what you need to do and what you want to do. Perhaps more time can be spent inside than doing the work you have been used to. No one is putting pressure on you, are they?"

"No. I am putting pressure on myself. Glenna, you are a wise young woman. I am getting ahead of myself. I am not used to being a man of leisure. I know I have to heal. I will take my time."

"That is so good to hear, Sen. Take all the time you need."

"I will and thank you."

"Do not be silly. You are family."

* * *

GLENNA STOOD in the doorway of the kitchen, watching the staff bustle around. She loved this time of year. They were all busy preparing for Hogmanay, and she could smell the delicious food cooking. She smiled and closed her eyes, savouring the moment. She had been taking the samples of the feast up to Molly, so she could try them. Molly would have preferred to be in the kitchen, but Alasdair would not allow it.

114

"He wants me to be fully rested for Hogmanay. I understand his concerns."

"So you should, Molly. The travelling from Edinburgh took more out of you than any of us realized. And you were on tenterhooks about the possibility of another attack. I understand your concern. But you need the rest both for yourself and the baby."

"I know. I just want to help."

Glenna smiled at her as she handed her the plate of biscuits for her to taste.

"These look interesting."

"They are. There is shortbread in circular shapes. There is your favorite chocolate chip. Mrs. Gillies loves making them. But this time she has made them square shaped. Don't they look different?"

"They do and I like the look."

"Try the jam drops. And then the chocolate oat cake."

"Mmm. They are all very nice."

"See? You can trust us to do it for you this year. Next year we expect you to come up with lots of different biscuit ideas."

"I am already making notes, see?" Molly lifted a small notebook off the table and handed it to Glenna.

"You really are bored."

"No not bored, not really."

"Alasdair wants to keep you safe. That's all."

"I know. I just hate feeling like an invalid. I guess I won't feel better till I know the queen is not coming back."

"Well, Blake did say she is under arrest in the future."

"But when will that occur. Boy every time I think of this time travel stuff my head hurts."

"Whatever happens, until we are sure we will not leave you alone. She will never hurt you again."

"I hope you are right. What about you? How do you feel."

"I feel good. I am at peace. I am sure that my time with

115

Sinclair has not come to an end. I love him and I know he loves me. I just have to wait and see what happens."

"I am so pleased to hear that. I hope to meet him soon."

"Yes. I hope for the same thing. Now, have a nap. We are having dinner together tonight and some time to sit and remember the year that was. And then tomorrow is Hogmanay eve. And midnight will be ready and waiting for us."

"Thank you, Glenna. You have been such a strength."

* * *

GLENNA WATCHED MOLLY SLEEP PEACEFULLY, her brow unfurrowed. She knew Molly needed her rest, and she was glad to be able to give it to her during the day. However, at night, she was always on edge. She knew Dair would never leave her side, but it was still when she was most vulnerable. It was when she felt in her heart the queen was lurking. Watching.

Glenna made her way downstairs. She had shared her thoughts on the topic with her brother and he had taken her concerns seriously. He had posted a servant outside their room with strict instructions to enter if they heard screaming or yelling. So far, the nights had been uneventful. She knew there was nothing to worry about, but she couldn't help but feel a sense of relief at the start of each new day. She closed her eyes and prayed the nights would stay quiet.

She entered the library to find Sen and Dair chatting.

"Is Molly asleep?"

"I have suggested she nap as we will be eating together tonight, and she needs the rest."

"Good. I will leave you to chat with your brother while I sit with her. It eases my mind to watch her sleep."

Sen offered her his seat and left the library, closing the door behind him.

"Sit down, sister. How are you?"

"I am in good spirits."

"Are you not concerned Sinclair has not yet arrived?"

"I am not. In fact, I am at peace. I know he will come. It is just a matter of when."

"I hope you are right. What do you think delays him?"

"If I know Sinclair and I think I do, he will be making sure the queen is taken care of for good."

"I hope you are right."

"I am at peace."

"Good. Now what of dinner tonight?"

"I just thought it would be nice to be all together before the excitement of the Hogmanay. We have not eaten together since Christmas Day."

"You are right. It will be good to sit together and not feel like we are on watch. Besides, the staff have their hands full getting ready for the event."

"True. I will rest myself before dinner." She got up and went and stood in front of her brother.

Dair stood and put his arms around her shoulders. "I am glad you are home."

"As am I, Dair. I feel the promise of a wonderful new year and do not wish to be anywhere else."

WHO'S GOT THE QUEEN?

*D*inner was wonderful. Everyone laughed and discussed the celebrations of Hogmanay. They then retired to the library where they put their feet up and waited for the tea to be brought in.

Glenna looked around at her family, all gathered together for a special occasion. They were laughing and talking, and she could feel the love and warmth in the room. She smiled, feeling content and grateful. She was so glad to be a part of this family. She wanted to share that feeling with Sinclair.

Molly had just made the comment 'she hated to feel like an invalid'. Dair was ready for her.

"May I remind you my dear, your arm is not fully healed and will appreciate the rest. Besides Mrs. Gillies sends you samples of everything that has been baked or cooked for the feast."

"That is true. I guess I just don't want to sit and do nothing." Molly frowned.

Glenna had to stop herself from giggling. "In a few short months you will be well and truly occupied when the bairn arrives."

"Okay. I get it. Enjoy the peace and quiet while I can."

From the shadows came a voice sending chills up Glenna's spine.

"I can kill ye and then ye cannot complain."

Immediately Dair was standing in front of Molly. Sen was behind her with his hand on her shoulder and Glenna grabbed her hand.

"Come out, you witch," Sen demanded.

Sebille stepped out into the light only six feet in front of Dair. She looked regal but something in her eyes gave Glenna the distinct impression she was not in her right mind. She looked deranged even maniacal. She had never judged anyone like that before and even now, knowing what she was capable of, was reluctant to do so.

"What do you want?" Molly asked.

"Your life, granddaughter."

"I do not know you nor do I see you as any relation of mine."

"That may be so but does not change the fact, I want you dead. Then no one can usurp me."

"Over my dead body," Dair declared.

The queen gave a chilling laugh. "Oh laird, we can easily arrange you dead." She lifted her hand and snaped her fingers. Two fae appeared from behind her and came and stood next to her.

"Now we can make this easy. Give Molly to me and no one will die."

Glenna stepped in front of Molly and next to Dair. "She is not going anywhere with you."

"Listen fae, you take orders from me. I am the queen."

"But you are not the queen," Glenna responded. "That title has been taken off you. And Molly has rejected it. So, leave."

"You will argue with your queen?"

"You are not my queen. You never will be."

The teal light filled the air.

"Sebille, you are no longer the queen. Stand aside." Blake

stepped out of the dark and stood in front of the queen and between her and Molly.

He addressed the other two fae.

"Fae, she has had her crown removed. Go back to the kingdom now or face the same punishment as the queen."

The two fae looked at each other then back at Blake. One lifted his hand to his heart and vanished, The other stepped forward. Blake jumped and had him in a neck brace in a moment.

Jake and the unnamed brother came from the dark and took the fae accomplice away.

"That will not stop me…" Sebille took a step toward Molly.

Suddenly, a teal blue light wrapped itself around the queen. She began to scream. "You cannot do this. I am the queen. She is not…"

The light faded and she was gone.

Blake turned to face the Murrays who stood there shaking their heads in total disbelief.

"She will not return. She was warned if she came here, she would be arrested and sentenced to death."

Molly came to stand before him. "And why death?"

"Because she tried to kill you and your father. The evidence against her was overwhelming. You will not be safe unless she is dead. If she lives, she will not stop trying to kill you."

"I did not ask for her death."

"No Molly, but as a guardian I did. I want to protect you and the baby. I have had enough as had many of the other fae. We did all we could to tell her she would die if she came back to you. She did not listen. Her mind was not in a good place."

"And what of her followers?"

"All have seen the error of their ways and have denounced the queen. We do not look kindly to those who would damage the relationships we have with humankind."

Dair wrapped his arms around Molly. "I will take you at your word, fae. I hope and pray we will never see her again."

"This is the last you will see of me as a fae. I promise. Live a long life you two. The fae thanks you." The teal light appeared and then disappeared, and he was gone.

Molly stood there holding on to her husband. "Is it really over?"

"It would seem so, darling Molly."

"Molly, as a fae I can promise you now, it is all over." Glenna put her arms around her and hugged her. "It is finally over. I know it in my heart."

"I believe you. Thank God."

Sen, Dair and she hugged Molly all together. "It is finally over."

Molly repeated. "It is over." And burst into tears.

* * *

DAIR HAD TAKEN Molly to bed, leaving Mrs Gillies to sit with her as she slept. He was pacing back and forth in front of the fireplace in the library.

"She has gone. I know. She is dead. The guardians have carried out the sentence."

"How can we be sure?"

Glenna stood and put her arms around her brother. "It is finished because I am fae and I know. We are all sad that a queen had to be put to death to protect the future queen. I do not know who she is but the fae have found her. I know here." She placed her hand on her heart.

Dair wrapped his arms around his sister and began to sob.

Glenna was heartbroken for her brother. The tension created since the guardians appeared on their wedding day had almost broken them. But she could be content to share her knowledge the queen was indeed dead. It was what the fae shared with each other. The knowledge that she, the queen, who had tormented the fae world and the human one was finally dead and could do no more harm.

Sen's voice drifted into her thoughts.

"Glenna is telling the truth. I feel it also. She is dead. She, who was once my mother, is no more."

Dair drew Sen into the hug. It was finally over. It was at that moment that the huge shadow, which had been hanging over them was finally gone.

HOGMANAY

The next day everyone in the house was excited and delighted that the eve of Hogmanay was finally with them. At around eight o'clock, after the evening meal had been eaten, the family gathered again in the library. Mrs. Boyce had added many more candles to the room, shedding light on every nook and cranny.

There was no need. Even Molly seemed happy and probably knew in her heart the queen had gone for good. Glenna knew Molly had not asked for a death sentence, nor had she but they both knew in their hearts the right course of action had been taken. Earlier in the day, Glenna had talked with Molly and both were at peace.

* * *

GLENNA WROTE in the journal of the event. She told Sinclair everything that happened and how they felt.

To know it is over is a great relief. Molly can now concentrate on her marriage to Alasdair and on the baby that is to come. As we prepare for Hogmanay, everything in the world feels right. Except that you and I are not yet reunited. I love you, dear Sinclair. I hope you can feel it.

She closed the journal and placed the pencil on the table. The journal was finished. She knew in her heart; she did not need to write anything else. She took it down to the library. She went and placed the journal next to the one from Alasdair. She had told her brother she was going to add her own diary. He would make sure it followed on from this time in his own diaries. One day she knew Sinclair would read it.

* * *

It was coming up to midnight and Glenna had never been more at peace and excited about the upcoming events. Staff and the family were gathered together in the foyer. Molly was rugged up and sitting in a chair. Hamish had arrived from Edinburgh earlier in the day. He slipped his hand into Glenna's. She gave it a squeeze.

"It is so good to have you home."

"It is good to be here. Though it seemed I missed out on the fun."

"Hardly fun, besides now as the new year is about to dawn, I believe we will have a lot less 'fun' as you say, to deal with."

"Oh Glenna, the year is just about to begin, and I believe you will be at the center of it."

"I do hope you are wrong. I think we have had enough. I personally look forward to a peaceful year."

Glenna placed her hand on the shoulder of Molly who sat in front of her.

"Hamish, leave your poor sister alone." Molly smiled up at them both.

Hamish grinned at Glenna, and she returned the cheeky grin.

Mrs. Boyce came and whispered in Molly's ear.

"All the fires in the fireplaces are out and cleaned. The ashes are buried in the garden."

"Thank you, Mrs. Boyce," Molly replied.

Glenna was excited. They agreed Molly should join Dair in opening the front door of the castle. She was now the lady. The two would open the door to the 'first foot'. The old year was over. The queen would not return. What joy would the new year hold?

This and many other thoughts ran through Glenna's mind. Rachael was happy with her Duncan, and baby Clara, in the future. Molly was here with her Dair in the past and expecting their own child. What of Hamish and even her own life?

Hamish had said to Molly that afternoon.

You cannot plan for others; you need to only be concerned for your life.

He was right, of course. Dear Hamish, was always right.

The clock began to chime. Molly stood up, still holding Dair's hand. Then the strikes came. One, two, three… They made their way to the door. Molly looked back at Hamish and her and smile at them. Four, five, six… There was no need for them to hurry. Seven, eight, nine…

"We must wait for the final strike before we open the door," said Alasdair. Ten, eleven, and twelve.

Dair place his hand on the door handle and opened it.

There stood a man she knew immediately. Molly and Dair however did not know him. Hamish squeezed her hand. She could feel the tears of joy flowing down her face.

He was tall like Dair. His hair was black as a raven. Oh, how she loved his black hair. He was about thirty years old. He had not aged a day since she last saw him. He was handsome also. Oh, so very handsome. In his arms he held a basket.

"I come bearing gifts, laird. May I enter?"

"Yes, you may. This is my wife, Molly."

"Lady Murray." He bowed.

"Enter stranger and take some rest." She bid him come in.

"I need no rest but bring gifts for your hospitality to me."

He placed the basket on the table in the foyer and more guests entered after him. Staff and family gathered around.

"I have shortbread. Also, some coal and wood to keep you warm. Here too, is a bottle of the finest whisky to welcome the new year. Some bread and salt. And lastly…" He handed Molly a silver rattle. "For the bairn, who is to come."

Molly hugged the stranger.

"Thank you, kind sir."

"Many thanks, stranger," Alasdair said.

"I am no stranger anymore. Call me Sinclair."

"Welcome, Sinclair. Welcome all. Let the festivities begin."

Sinclair made his way to Glenna and took her into his arms. He kissed her long and hard as the sounds of cheers and hoots of joy echoed through the space around them.

"I love you, Glenna." And he kissed her again.

MARRY ME

"I knew you would come. I love you."

"Dearest Glenna, I love you so. Thank you for the diary. It led me here to you, this day."

Glenna was laughing but it was from the joy that filled her heart.

"I only placed it with Dair's diaries this morning. And now here you are."

He kissed her again. Cheers and hoots of joy still surrounded them.

"Introduce me, sister," Hamish said as he placed his hands on her shoulder.

"Hamish, this is Sinclair. He is from the future."

"But planning to live in the past," Sinclair added.

"With the way you were kissing my sister just then, I will be holding you to that declaration."

"I am happy for you to do so." He put out his hand and Hamish shook it. "I am delighted to meet you. Glenna has told me so much about you."

"Sinclair, I am so happy you have arrived. Glenna never gave up on you." Alasdair put out his hand and Sinclair shook it.

"Laird Murray, I am delighted to meet you at last."

"You are family, Sinclair, you can call me Alasdair."

"It would appear, I am the only one who does not know you or of you. But if you make my Glenna happy, I too am pleased to meet you."

Molly came up and hugged Glenna. "This is fantastic. We are together and have no need to worry about the queen. Sinclair is here and all will be well."

Sinclair raised an eyebrow as he looked at Glenna.

"I will fill you in later. But for now, we should join in with all the clan and celebrate like we have never celebrated before."

They joined in the throng. Glenna beamed with pride as she introduced Sinclair to her friends and family. She couldn't wait for everyone to meet the man she loved. She held his hand tightly, her eyes sparkling with excitement.

* * *

"The library is amazing. So similar to the future but distinctly different here in the past. I wonder if I will ever get used to it."

Glenna hugged him. "I hope you will."

He returned the hug. "Do not fret my love, I am not going anywhere."

Alasdair handed him a glass of whisky. "Is this where I speak up and say, 'what are your intentions with my sister?'"

He took the glass. "Thank you. Well, I was going to wait till later but now seems it might be the right time." He dropped to one knee, took Glenna by the hand, raised his glass and asked, "Will you marry me, sweet Glenna?"

She dropped to her knees in front of him and declared, "Yes."

"Hurray." And he downed the whisky with one gulp and then kissed her.

He tasted of the whisky, and she deepened the kiss. He tasted so good. He responded by taking her in his arms and leaning into her kiss all the more.

"Very well, young ones. You are hereby engaged," Alasdair announced.

Glenna felt the heat rise to her face as she watched Sinclair glow red.

It was late in the evening, well early morning. Molly had already gone to bed and Dair and Hamish had stayed around while Glenna filled Sinclair and Hamish in on the previous day's event. Sinclair knew only a little from the diary. The proposal did feel right, surrounded by her brothers who she knew had no intention of leaving her alone until a declaration had been made. Now it had, Dair announced he was going to bed. She would have to fill Molly in with a description of the event.

"I will speak with you more on the morrow."

"Yes, Alasdair." And Sinclair bowed.

"No need of the formality. Our family is very much complete now you have arrived. Glenna, make sure he has a room in the family wing."

"Yes, Dair. I have already spoken to Mrs. Boyce."

"Good girl. Goodnight, all." And Dair made his way to the stairs leaving the door of the library open.

"I too, will bid you goodnight. Do not stay up long as we will have lots to discuss tomorrow."

"Yes, Hamish. I am just waiting on Mrs. Boyce to tell me which room Sinclair will be staying in."

"Goodnight." And he too departed leaving the door open.

Sinclair and Glenna sat on the sofa.

"They are very protective of you."

"Yes, I am their little sister. What do you expect?"

"I can honestly say I don't know. As I have no family, I have no idea."

"Do not worry, you will learn a lot over the coming days as they drag out every bit of information out of you as they can."

Mrs. Boyce came in.

"Mrs. Boyce, you are the first to know, we are engaged."

"Congratulations Miss Glenna, and welcome to the family Sinclair…"

"Murray-Green."

"Oh, how lovely another Murray. I have placed you in Alasdair's old room if that is convenient, Miss Glenna."

"It is, Mrs. Boyce. Thank you."

She stood and took Sinclair by the hand, and they headed upstairs as Mrs. Boyce extinguished the candles and collected the empty glasses.

They walked to the door of Dair's old room, and she kissed him goodnight.

"Tomorrow, we talk about a wedding date. I want you in my bed as soon as possible." He laid a gentle kiss on her lips, then opened the door and went into the room. She floated to her room. Well, that was the way it felt to her. Candles still lit the hallway leading to her room. The end of the greatest day of her life.

WHAT WILL I DO AND HOW WILL
WE LIVE?

*B*reakfast was late and the family were all together. To have Glenna by his side took his breath away. As did being in the past. He would have to learn to dress differently as well as do a job of some sort. There were so many questions he needed answers to.

The butler gave him a plate of scrambled eggs and ham. He very tentatively tasted it and then started to devour it. The food tasted wonderful.

"Mrs. Gillies, will want to hear your thoughts."

He stopped and looked at Glenna. "Reading my mind again, are we?"

"She does that a lot," Molly added. "But be warned, so do I."

"It just isn't safe around here, is it?"

"Only if we are fae. And you need not complain. I understand you are capable of the same."

"Oh, he is fae, too. I am learning a great deal about you, young Sinclair." Hamish laughed and the others joined in. "Tell us your story."

So, he did. Talking with his new family filled him with both excitement and joy. He had never experienced this before. With his re-found memories of the fae family he had; he now knew he had been an only child. He loved to joke around with Hamish and Alasdair seemed to enjoy his company also. This boded well.

"You could not remember your adopted family at all?" Alasdair asked.

"No, not till I asked the guardians to give me back my memories."

"Say what you will Glenna, Blake and his brothers have a great deal to answer for."

"I agree, brother, but now you have a future with your love Molly, and Duncan has Rachael and Clara. All we want is to have our chance." She smiled at him, and his heart jumped for joy.

"I want Glenna and I, to have our happy ever after. Does that make sense? I want to marry Glenna as soon as we can and begin to have a life I had only dreamed of."

"We had only dreamed of. We both want this. You see, for years now I have been concerned about the fae and carrying on the stories and the history of our mother. Then Duncan met Rachael and I did all I could to bring them together."

"And then you did the same for us," Molly added.

"Yes. But I have no regrets. I wanted the happiness I could see in you both to come forth. But now, I know what love can do for me. And I want Sinclair more than anything else."

"And I want to be with Glenna, forever. I have never felt this way before."

"I want to help you both find a future. But what is it that you want?" Alasdair was serious.

"I want to continue to be the fae representative for the family. I owe you all that much."

"And you, Sinclair, what is it you think you can do?" Alasdair asked.

"May I intrude in this conversation?" Sen looked at Alasdair.

"You are a valued member of the family, Sen, please tell us your thoughts."

"I have been weakened by the attack on my person. Continuing as the manager of this estate requires a set of younger hands. If you would allow me to retire, laird, I could train up Sinclair to manage the estate for you. This would allow me to continue to be a guardian of Molly, if you would allow me, and also be able to help and enjoy the young family that will come."

Sinclair looked at Sen and then to Alasdair.

"What do you think, Sinclair? Could this interest you?" Alasdair questioned.

"Truthfully laird…"

"Please call me Alasdair. You are family now. Remember?"

"I would love to do as Sen has suggested. The land and the growth of the plants and the animals is part of me, part of being a Ghillies Dhu. Looking after them is a part of my being."

Alasdair pondered these words for a moment. Then finally he spoke.

"I want Glenna to remain the fae ambassador of the family. I want her to teach Molly the history of her people as well as pass on the wisdom to both our children and her own. Her wisdom can be written down and shared for future generations. I am thinking Duncan and Rachael would want this also. Then I suggest you and Sen begin the transfer of powers and administration. I know you will learn much from my father-in-law."

"Thank you, Alasdair. This is an honour I gladly accept."

Glenna jumped to her feet and threw her arms around Dair. "Thank you, brother. This all feels right."

Hamish added. "Agreed, mother would be so excited to know her legacy will continue."

Molly stood and waited. "I want to add my excitement to this plan. But we have one more question that needs an answer. When will you marry?"

Glenna came and placed her arms around her sister-in-law.

"Thank you, Molly. I feel I have been part of everyone else's story, but now I have the chance to see my dreams come true."

"Well?"

"It is true we want to marry soon but for me I want the sun to be shining when we do."

He stood and came and placed his arms around her. "Then a summer wedding it will be."

"Let us all return at luncheon and make plans for all we have discussed. We need to also work out where you will live." Dair and Molly left the room and Hamish came and hugged his sister.

"We can sort all of this out over the coming days. I am excited for you both. I will see you at luncheon." He hugged them both and left.

Sen came over. "I knew you would be the right person to take my place, the moment you arrived. I knew you were fae and a Ghillies Dhu."

"Thank you, Sen. It is a wonderful idea."

Glenna hugged him. "Thank you."

Sen departed the room. Glenna placed her arms around him, and he could not think of any place he would rather be, than here with his love.

* * *

GLENNA WAS SITTING on the sofa with a pad of paper and a pencil in hand. The library was warm and cosy as they made notes for the luncheon meeting. Glenna's eyes sparkled as she gazed at the snow-covered landscape. She took a deep breath of the crisp, cold air and smiled. She was home with her love, and everything was perfect.

"Are you happy for me to be the manager of the estate?" Sinclair asked.

"But of course, my dear. It is the perfect job for you. But will you be happy?"

"I believe so. I want to ask Dair if he will allow me to also maintain the library. I love to research, and I can gather the family's history and make it a special collection for the family and for Scotland."

"Oh, my dearest, that is such a wonderful idea. I am sure Dair will agree. And Hamish will help you to obtain the books you will want and need to make the library even more a beautiful resource."

"Then you are happy for me to do so? I would like to include your fae history."

"But of course. You can tell me what you want, and I will happily write it all down. We already know it is what Alasdair wants."

She watched him slip into deep thought. His brow creased.

"What are you thinking?"

"Strange you are asking and not just looking."

"I will always ask." She smiled.

He took her hand and gave it a squeeze. She did love the feel of her hand in his.

"I was wondering why we did not find these resources in the future."

She thought for a moment. "I would think it is because we are here now. We do not plan to go back to the future. It is a decision that affects us now. It is our future that we are beginning. We had not thought about it in the future."

He still had hold of her hand and gave it another squeeze. "I think I understand. You are wise. Time travel does give you a headache at times."

"Yes, I think all of us would agree with that."

"Where then will we live? The big house or the castle if you prefer is Molly's and Alasdair's home."

"We can check with Sen if he is happy for us to take his house, the manager's cottage. I can ask Dair if we can enlarge it and make more suitable for a family."

"That is a great idea. There is a manager's office here in the castle too, is it not?"

"Yes, and you could do your research there also. We could have a small library at home where we could both work on the research."

Glenna got up and rang the bell. A footman came in and she asked for tea to be brought in. Again, he was deep in thought. She watched as a crease appeared on his brow. That was his deep in thought look.

"You have been used to having servants. What shall we do? What is it that you would want? And is it right for me to have some? I am not sure of our social standing."

"I guess I had not thought about it. We are family of the castle, so we are entitled. But I do like to cook since I have spent time with Rachael and Molly. Perhaps we could have one maid who can help me with the whole house. Especially as we will both be working."

"Perhaps we can decide what we need once we have determined where we are to live. Let us concentrate on a few of the wedding plans."

"Can you wait till the summer?" she asked tentatively.

"Yes, dear Glenna. We are to be wed. I will wait for summer. I like the idea of a summer wedding. Do you wish for a church wedding?"

"No. I mean, I want the parish minister to perform the service but the great oak, where Molly and Dair were wed, would seem the perfect place. It is a tradition I would like to maintain."

"The reverend, is he aware of the fae in the family?"

"Oh yes. You cannot keep something like that away from any member of the clan. And he is a member of the clan."

"I would like it to be a traditional service from this period."

"Agreed. Who would you like to stand as your best man?"

"Hamish, if he would. We seem to have a fondness for each other."

"Yes. Hamish is excited you are fae. It is what he had hoped for me. He told me last night."

"Who will you have as your maids?"

"I would rather not have any. In fact, why not have just Hamish. I do not want the pressure on Molly as she may give birth either just before or just after the wedding."

"Very well."

They enjoyed the cuppa that had been brought in. She watched him and he was still deep in thought. She smiled to herself. Never had she thought she could be this happy. Her adult life had been so centered on her brothers. And now she had the chance to be as happy as they were. It all seemed too good to be true. But the queen was dead, and life would go back to some kind of normalcy. At least that is what she hoped.

LUNCHEON

The family were all gathered again. Glenna placed the
pad of paper on the table next to her. She was home
with her Sinclair and so very happy. Everyone spoke with ease, as
they ate their meal.

"I want to share some thoughts if I may."

"Of course, brother. You are the laird."

"I may be laird, but I am your brother and I want for you to
feel part of this family. This is your home. I want what is right for
both of you. If Sen will allow, I would like to expand the manager's quarters for your use, as a family. I have another suggestion
for Sen."

"We were going to ask that of you. But we did not want to
displace Sen."

"Sen, we want you to be part of the family also. You are
Molly's da, after all. Can we give you a cottage of your own but
have your meals with us, in the main house? I want you to have
the privacy you have had for many years but also the chance to
spend as much time as you can with your daughter."

Sen was looking at his hands in his lap.

"I am delighted I have found Molly. She is my daughter and I wish to remain near her if you will allow. I promised to be her guardian and I wish to keep that promise. A small cottage I can call my own would be most welcome. I can maintain a garden and continue to help with the vegetable garden, if the new manager will allow." He looked at Sinclair and smiled.

Sinclair nodded.

"That is good. We will start immediately on the plans to expand the manager's house for you both to move into after your wedding. Till then you can stay here with us."

She looked at Sinclair and smiled.

"Dair, may we suggest something?"

"Of course, Glenna."

"Both Sinclair and I would like to continue to write and develop the family history. It is Sinclair's forte. In fact, it would be mainly his job. I would help on the fae history."

"A wonderful idea, Glenna," Hamish said. "I could get all the books and items you would need to do the job."

"Agreed. Sinclair, there is a manager's office in the castle so we can all stay close and help you with the history. But it is your expertise in the area which makes you the right person for the job. You can start using the office when you are ready to do so. Glenna, I agree the fae history of the family needs to be maintained. We will do as you have suggested."

"Thank you, brother."

"You need to live well as the leader of the fae in the family. Do you not agree, Sen?"

"Wholeheartedly."

"I may be fae and the lady of the estate but you, dear Glenna, are the first fae of the Murray clan, the direct ancestor of your mother. It has to be your position."

"Dear Molly, you know my heart and you know the heart of my sister. You have without my even asking recognized her position in the family. Glenna, the house will also have a cook and two maids. I want you to feel you are still at home."

"That is very generous of you, dear Dair."

"Not at all. We are family. More so than we have been for many years. Sinclair, let us get together after luncheon and deal with some of the plans."

Sinclair looked at his Glenna and nodded.

* * *

HE WAS AT PEACE, and the past and Glenna were what he wanted. He hoped there would be no problems with his uncles, the guardians. But he did not want to think about them. Once they had the plans in place, he would call them, and invite them to the wedding.

He listened to Alasdair as they went over the plan of the old cottage. He penciled in the extra rooms they would need and areas for family gatherings. He would not always want to go to the castle but would still want to gather the whole family in each other's homes.

"Have you forgiven my uncles and their interference?"

Dair looked him in the eyes and for a moment he felt uncomfortable. But that was only a moment. Dair was smiling and he continued to look into his eyes.

"You are nothing like them if you were wondering. They felt they needed to take control of the situation. I understand. But they do have a tendency to look down their noses at us, as if we are the ones causing the problem."

"I must admit I am frightened as to when they will suddenly appear, as if they had been listening to my conversation all the time. It is unnerving. And you don't know what they will say or do next."

He looked around waiting to see if they would appear because he dared to mention them. Dair began to laugh, and he joined in.

"I am glad you are here for Glenna."

140

"I love her. From the moment I saw her I was attracted to her. We have a connection which is hard to explain."

"I understand. It was similar with Molly and me. I fell for her almost immediately. It is hard to explain. Now, I cannot imagine life without her."

He nodded, pleased his future brother-in-law could open up with him. He was not like his brother Duncan. They may have similar features, but Dair seemed more gregarious than Duncan. He missed Duncan but felt Dair and he would be good friends.

"We need to wait for the snow to lift, before we get serious about the additions, but we can order the materials and have anything else we need sent from Edinburgh."

"That sounds wonderful. And thank you for your trust in me. I think I will like managing the land."

"I am sure it is right. But I want to include you in more of the family plans. Rachael helped us extend our influence in the area with many new ideas. Some we have acted on, others we still need to do some work and planning. But with some aspects of your future knowledge, I believe we will succeed in our expansions."

"I will be glad to do what I can."

"Good." He slapped him gently on the back and they returned to the plans on the table.

WHAT DO YOU WANT, GLENNA?

The sun's light, mottled by the grey clouds, drifted into the window. She was awake. The maid had opened the curtain and had announced that Mistress Molly would arrive shortly with her morning cuppa. She sat up and got out of bed. Placing her dressing gown on, she went to the fireplace and stoked the wood into flame. She just sat down at the table near the window when Molly entered followed by a maid carrying a tray with teacups and alike.

"I thought it would be nice to have a cuppa together."

"I have missed our mornings together. But what about you and Dair? Do you not have a cuppa with him in the mornings now?"

"It is true we have done that since just before we married. But on this occasion, I felt the need to arrange something different for you."

"That sounds intriguing."

"Oh Glenna, it is. But first let us have a drink." Molly acted as mother and poured the tea and then sat down.

"Today we will remember what you and I shared. This cuppa and our friendship. But we will be entering a new stage in both our lives. I am to have a babe and you, my dearest friend, will be married. And perhaps in the future, children will be in your gift."

She nodded. So much had changed since they first started having cuppas together. She picked up her cup and drank. Leaning back into the chair she sighed. The first taste of tea in the morning was so refreshing. It always made her feel good.

"I have missed this but what is it you have planned?"

"Well, I enjoyed having the start of the day with Dair. He can be busy and so will Sinclair as he takes on the role of estate manager."

There was a knock at the door.

"Come."

The maid came in with another tray and fresh tea. Following her in was Sinclair looking baffled as to why he was here.

"Ah, Sinclair. Come and sit down." Molly stood, cup in hand and stepped aside for Sinclair. He sat. "Start as you mean to go with my dearest friend." And she turned and left the room, followed by the maid and her empty tray.

"Do you know what she is talking about?"

"Yes, my dear. You see she and I used to start the day with a cuppa together. When I went to the future, she missed my company, but Dair then went in each morning and had a cuppa with her. She wants us to do the same. Start the day with each other. A very inspiring idea."

"I like the way she thinks." He poured himself a cup of tea. "But would you mind if in future I have coffee?"

"Of course not. Dair is the same. He has his morning coffee too."

"How did you sleep, my dear?" he asked, leaning back in the chair and smiling.

"Very well. You and Dair tackled a lot yesterday. How do you feel about the various changes?"

"Good. I like the idea of being in charge of the land. The soil is in my blood. Your brother trusts me and of that I am grateful."

"I trust you. I know that Dair will if I do but you have proven yourself over the last days with your ideas and plans. I have no doubt you will flourish here."

"I will if you are by my side."

She could feel the creep of heat, up her neck and face.

"I mean it. We knew each other almost from the moment we met."

"Even though I was angry at you. Yelling and accusing."

"Yes. Your feistiness grabbed me and would not let me go. But your role from here on, will you be happy?"

"Oh, my darling Sinclair. It is what I live for. Being the fae representative has been my job for as long as I remember." She got up and sat on his lap. I want to be your love and the family fae. The fact you are fae gives me incredible joy. Our children..."

"Our children." He leaned in and kissed her. For that moment she was gone. Not because of just the kiss but dreaming of having his children filled her with such excitement.

"I want to take you to bed and practice making babies."

She laughed but with joy because she wished the same. "I promise we will do a lot of practice. I long to be in your arms."

"Just what I want to hear."

She had no doubt as she felt his erection very clearly. His hand gentle, he cupped her breast. He leaned down and kissed it. "You are mine, forever."

They were kissing again, and she too wanted this.

He stopped the kiss, resting his head on her shoulder. "We will meet each morning, before and after we wed. Just know I will have you in my bed when we wed, and I cannot promise I will be able to restrain myself. But for now, we must. We will honor each other. I love you, my dear." He stood, with her still in his arms, kissed her again and Glenna wished it would not stop. But he finally did stop and left the room.

* * *

GLENNA WAS glad to be dressed and going down to breakfast. If she had stayed in her room any longer, she might never have come out. The whole idea of being married to Sinclair consumed her. In a really wonderful way.

"Good morning, sister."

"Good morning, Dair. I want to get married sooner rather than later."

She looked at Sinclair who had shock written all over his face.

"Well, a great deal of the family and clan are still here, we could do it in the next few days…"

"Why the rush?" Molly asked.

Glenna smiled at her dear friend and watched her composed expression change. Her face reddened and she chuckled.

"But I thought you wanted a spring/summer wedding?" Sinclair asked.

She smiled at her dearest Sinclair.

"I want you more." Now, he too was going red. "I just don't know if I want to wait."

"But the snow is thick on the ground. It would be difficult to marry under the oak."

"I know." She sat down and the footman placed her breakfast in front of her.

Sinclair was looking at her. He was concerned. She had said nothing to him and just blurted out what she wanted. She began to regret her ability to ignore convention.

"What do you really want?" he asked her, not taking his eyes from hers.

"I want you." A truer thing she had never said before.

"And I want you. What do you want to do?"

"Marry you and be with you forever."

"You will be."

Molly was crying. "Give me till tomorrow and I will get all in place. Is that soon enough?"

Glenna looked into Sinclair's eyes and together they said, "Yes."

"Done. You shall be wed tomorrow." Alasdair stood and came and shook Sinclair's hand. Everyone was standing and hugging and kissing each other. The day was going to be long. There was going to be a wedding.

ANOTHER WEDDING

*M*olly sat with Mrs. Gillies and Mrs. Boyce. They were taking notes and organizing a storm. Glenna slowly left the kitchen and went back up the hall to the foyer. Servants were dashing here and there. The atmosphere had an energy she had never seen before.

"Having regrets?"

"No, just amazed how everyone can stay focused once they make up their mind what to do. Do you have regrets?"

"Not on your life. I want you and always will."

He took her in his arms, and he kissed her long and hard.

"I will be glad to be with you forever and we can start early if that is what you want."

"It is. Now, if you will excuse me, I have a fitting for my dress. The maids are waiting for me in my room."

"Then I will let you go. Can't wait to see you in it tomorrow."

She made her way upstairs to her bedroom. Eileen, Molly's maid, was there, and two other young maids. And on the bed was her mother's wedding dress. The gems sent beads of light all over the room. She remembered Molly in the dress only months ago.

They were similar in size so she hoped little alteration would be needed.

"A nip and tuck here and there and it will be beautiful. Oh, to think it will be worn by you, miss. Your mother would have been delighted."

She thought about her mother and the fact she was not here to see her in the dress. In her mind and thoughts, she hoped her mother would know. And her da too. She picked up the dress and watched the dancing lights bouncing off the wall.

"I do hope so, Eileen. I want her to be proud."

"No question of that, miss. She would be the proudest. Mr. Sinclair is a fine man and your ma and da would be proud as punch."

She took off her clothes and put on the dress. Eileen started doing up the buttons on the back. Then she stood back and looked at her.

Not a thing to be done, miss. Is it comfortable for you?"

"It is, Eileen. I am pleased. I did not want you up all night getting it ready."

"No need to worry about that, miss. Seems the dress had its own ideas. Now, you get changed and we will freshen it up, so it is ready for tomorrow."

She did what she was told and then the maids left. Seemed all was going well. She stood still and looked around her, and began to laugh. She had half expected the guardians to pop out of the walls and ruin her day. But they did not. Small mercies.

* * *

AT DINNER that night everything and everybody were buzzing with excitement.

"The dress is ready and wait till you see, Sinclair. She will be stunning in her outfit." Molly was grinning from ear to ear.

She saw Sinclair blush red, but he was smiling so she knew he was enjoying himself.

"I will give you away, if I may?" Dair piped in.

"Of course, Dair, I would love that."

"And I will be the best man for Sinclair."

"An honor I accept with gratitude, Ham."

"Ham?"

"Yes, your beloved thinks the nick name suits me."

"You will never live that down, brother dear."

Molly continued her report. "The food is all sorted, and the actual wedding will take place..."

"Do not tell her," Dair said. "She can find out tomorrow. At the appointed time, I will meet you in the kitchen."

She looked from person to person, but it was clear she would not get any further information from anyone.

"Very well. The kitchen it is."

"Now, the service will be at three, so you all know your places. Then after the service we will have dinner in the dining room and in the hallway. We have a few other surprises but that can wait."

"Thank you, Molly. I know it was sudden but..."

"This is so much better. I have the energy now and might not come spring. Besides you need to be together."

In her mind she knew Molly was right. She had to be with her Sinclair.

* * *

"I AM grateful for all the family has done."

"In less than twenty-four hours they have pulled everything together."

She stopped halfway up the stairs and took his hand. "I want this to happen now. I am sorry I am impatient."

"I am not. This is what I want, too. I love you and want to be

149

with you. The sooner the better." He leaned over and gave her a gentle kiss on the lips.

They continued up the stairs holding hands. She left him at his door and headed to her room. Tomorrow there will be no more goodnights and going their separate ways. Tomorrow they will finally be together.

Glenna undressed and slipped into bed. She remembered little until she woke up screaming.

A SCREAM THAT DID NOT STOP

Glenna was sitting up in bed surrounded by members of the family when he came in. Tears were streaming down her face.

"Sinclair," she cried.

"What is wrong, my love?" He sat on the bed next to her. The butler came in with a cup of tea and handed it to her.

"I had a bad dream."

"What could be so bad to upset you so?"

"I dreamt the queen was leaning over my bed with a knife in her hand."

"The queen is dead, Glenna. The guardians assured us of it."

"Sinclair, look at her hands." Molly pleaded.

He did and they were covered in blood. Candles were being lit by servants and Mrs. Boyce had a bowl of warm water and rags. She made her way to Glenna's side and began to administer to her wounds.

"Someone attacked her." Molly wept.

He stood and yelled Blake's name. It was a yell full of anger and he wanted to wrap his hands around Blake's neck.

The teal light appeared, and Blake stood at the door. He rushed forward to Glenna.

"What on earth has happened?"

Sinclair grabbed his uncle's arm. "The queen? Where is she?"

"She is dead."

"Then who did this to Glenna and why? She is no threat."

"I shall return."

The light appeared and Blake was gone.

"Blast. I hate their vanishing tricks." Alasdair had his hands on his hips.

"As do I." Sinclair added.

"Her hands are not too bad," Mrs. Boyce declared. "She has a few nicks on the side of her hands. Whoever did this was not trying to damage her badly. They are smaller nicks than I would have thought."

She completed wrapping bandages around her hands and took the bowl away.

The teal light appeared again. This time Alasdair grabbed Blake.

"No more vanishing, guardian. Tell us what the hell is going on?"

"It was my brother Jake. He was arrested and taken to the council of fae. He says he wanted to scare you, Glenna."

"But why. What am I to him?"

"He believes the queen should not have died and the new queen is too young and inexperienced to be queen."

"Then you have gone to the future to get the real queen?" Sinclair asked.

"What are you saying…" Glenna was weeping.

"I wanted to wait till after the wedding to tell you how things will be."

Glenna leaned back into her pillows. Molly lay on the other side of her bed cradling one of Glenna's damaged hands. Hamish and Alasdair stood at the end of the bed. Sen had pulled up a chair from the table near the window and sat on the chair by the side of the bed near Molly.

Sinclair nestled next to Glenna, cradling her other bandaged hand in his as he sat next to her.

"I think it is time you tell us all, uncle," he said without pomp or ceremony. The other men took chairs and pulled them up near Glenna's bed.

"The queen is from the future. I do not wish to say who—other than she will be a direct descendant of you, Molly. You and Alasdair."

Molly placed her hand on her stomach.

"No. That is your son."

She smiled at Alasdair. "Little Dunks." Sinclair saw Alasdair smiling at his wife, a tear rolling down his cheek.

"I will not say anymore. Other than the queen will fall in love with my other brother, the nameless brother. He does not need to be nameless anymore. His name is Drake, and he will become the queen's consort and husband."

"What has Jake got to do with this and why hurt Glenna?" He was getting impatient.

"Jake wanted to scare Glenna so she would not marry and run back to the future. He does not believe in love, nor can he recognize the love you and Sinclair have for each other. You see, you will guide and direct the children of your own family and the family of Molly and Alasdair in the history and capabilities of the fae. You, Glenna, will teach the queen. You just will not know for some time who she will be. There will be a few girls in both sides of the family."

"I will teach her?"

"Yes, and the books you write on the family history, will play a very large part of the road all the children will take. Jake wanted to change the history of our queen. But he has been stopped. He has asked for forgiveness and realizes his error of judgement. The queen has forgiven him. It is up to you if you forgive him."

"I forgive him if he comes to the wedding and asks my forgiveness himself."

"We will be there. Jake, Drake and me. The queen wishes to stay in the background until the time is right."

"I understand."

Everyone looked at Blake.

"It is over. There is no more disagreement. All fae have given their allegiance to the new queen. Forgive me, Glenna."

"Please hear me uncle, you have said this before. If anything happens to my family, including all the Murrays now or in the future, I will find you and you will regret it."

"I believe you, Sinclair. But all is well." He bowed and the teal light came and went.

"Do you want to wait a day or two for the wedding?" Molly asked tentatively.

"No." Sinclair and Glenna's voice said in unison.

"I am even more determined now," Glenna added.

"As am I."

Alasdair helped Molly up off the bed and took his wife back to their room. Hamish came and whispered in Sen's ear and then left with him.

Sinclair closed the door behind them and began to put out the candles. He stoked the fire and grabbed a rug from the end of the bed.

"You are staying?" she asked, her eyebrows raised.

"Yes. I would not leave you alone despite the promises made."

He lay next to her on top of the covers, wrapping the rug around him.

"But..."

"But nothing. Tomorrow, we wed, and we will delight in consummating our marriage. But tonight, I will hold you in my arms and not allow anything to hurt you again. Your brother gave his permission without my need to ask. I am your guardian and will always be so."

She snuggled into him and quickly fell asleep. Holding her all night without making love to her was the hardest and most rewarding thing he could do for her and himself. The love of this woman was all he could dream of.

THE WEDDING

Glenna awoke in Sinclair's arms. It felt so good to be doing so. Today they would marry. Sinclair stirred. He sat up, kissed her gently on the mouth and got up.

"I will see you shortly, my love, for our morning cuppa," he said and left her room.

She had slept soundly in his arms. She felt safe and that was a good thing. Glenna had fought Jake off and was proud of her own bravery, but resting in Sinclair's arms was the peace she needed in her heart. And last night she had peace in abundance.

Moments later the maid and footman brought in her and Sinclair's morning cuppas. Her tea and his coffee. Just as they were leaving, Sinclair returned in his dressing gown. He came over to the bed and helped her get into her dressing gown and guided her to the chair and table near the window.

"It snowed heavily last night. How are you feeling?"

"I am fine, Sinclair. Thank you for staying with me last night."

"It was my pleasure. I wanted you to feel safe."

"And I did. Thank you."

They drank the tea and coffee which was provided.

"You didn't need me, but I was glad to help."

"Oh no. I needed you. More than you might know. You gave me peace and I slept soundly knowing I was in your arms. And that is the way I want it to be."

"And as from tonight, you will be there always."

"How could I not be happy and delighted?"

"Let us go to breakfast my dear, and then we can get ready for our wedding."

"A wonderful idea. I will dress and meet you there."

He stood and kissed her and went to change.

* * *

WHAT DO you do on your wedding day? It was a question she had asked herself a few times before today. Now, she was noting down all the events in her mind so she could write in her journal later. The journal with the G. Today as her new life began, she would start in a new journal. Yes, she would keep a journal just like Dair had. And by writing down her thoughts she might give her descendants and her brother Duncan a chance to know her better.

A light breakfast was at hand when she went downstairs. And that was all she felt like. Butterflies filled her stomach. Not real ones of course, but definitely felt like light fluttering wings in her tummy.

After breakfast she spent the morning having a bath, washing and drying her hair. Her maid, a present from her brother, did her hair. Jenny was younger than she but only by a year. The girl decorated her hair with flowers from the hot house. Mainly daisies. Along with the gems of the dress she would sparkle when presented to her husband. Sinclair would love it.

She had a light luncheon in her room and then rested on the bed for a while surrounded by cushions, so she didn't mess her hair. It was a day of calm after a night that had terrorized her. Mrs. Boyce came and rewrapped and treated her cuts. After carefully bandaging them, she wove ribbons around her hands to make them look decorated rather than bandaged. She even wove a few daisies into the ribbon. And now she was about to go downstairs via the kitchen to see what her family had planned as she married the man of her dreams. Sounded strange, but she wanted nothing else.

* * *

Glenna made her way down the back stairs to the kitchen. Alasdair was waiting for her. He wore a big smile but was also shining in a dark blue velvet coat. It perfectly matched the ancient Murray kilt that her father had worn. He was so handsome, and she was proud that he could give her away.

"Glenna, you look beautiful. Mother would…"

"Be proud, just as proud as when Molly wore the dress. It is a family heirloom, and I am delighted and proud myself to be wearing it."

He drew her into his arms and hugged her. She was glad to have Dair here and hoped Duncan would be happy at his brother taking on the job of giving her away.

"Are you ready?"

"Yes. You look stunning by the way."

"Then let us go through to the foyer."

"The foyer?"

"Yes. Molly has outdone herself."

She felt her eyebrow lift. The foyer seemed a strange place.

The two footmen opened the double doors that lead into the foyer. A wall of roses and their fragrance hit her as she came through the doorway. Vases of all shapes and sizes were filled with roses and daisies. The room was swimming in the sweet fragrance that danced around the room. Maids and clan members, footman and villagers were scattered in and around the vases. At the front door was the pastor from the Kirk in the village, who had married Molly and Dair. Next to him stood her Sinclair, with Hamish just behind. All around her were family and friends. Even Sinclair's uncles. They stood on the stairwell looking down at her with big smiles on their faces. Blake, Jake and now the named brother who was to marry the future queen, Drake.

Her eyes went back to her beloved. He wore the same dark blue coat as Dair did. Yet, he wore a different kilt with redder stripes in it. It must be his family's kilt. The coat matched it perfectly. His black raven hair, shining in the sunlight that came from the windows around the doorway. He was so handsome. She heard music. Four violins played Vivaldi Four Seasons, one of her favorite pieces of music. Marrying a man who loved nature and the land, it was a perfect piece to pick.

Alasdair stopped in front of the pastor.

"Who gives this bride away?"

"I do, gladly," her brother announced.

"And I would gladly take her," Sinclair proclaimed. He reached out his hand and she placed her fingers on the tips of his. He took her whole hand and drew her close to him.

"Become my wife, my darling."

"Become my husband, my dear."

He reached into his pocket and pulled out a piece of tartan. It was red with threads of blue and green crisscrossing the red. It matched the tartan he was wearing. It was his family tartan. On the piece was a broach with a heart and two knives laying down in front of the heart.

"I make ye a part of the Murray Green clan. My love is laid out before ye."

From her brother's pocket came a piece of the Murray tartan. The blue and green stripes with thin threads of red running through it. The pin connected was that of a sword. She took it in her hand.

"I make ye part of the Murray clan. My love is laid out

before ye."

"Master Sinclair, take Miss Glenna's hand and please repeat the words of your vows after me.

You are the star of each night,

You are the brightness of every morning," the pastor said.

"You are the star of each night,

You are the brightness of every morning,"

"You are the story of each guest,

You are the report of every land."

"You are the story of each guest,

You are the report of every land."

"No evil shall befall you, on hill nor bank,

In field or valley, on mountain or in glen."

"No evil shall befall you, on hill nor bank,

In field or valley, on mountain or in glen."

"Neither above, nor below, neither in sea,

Nor on shore, in skies above, Nor in the depths."

"Neither above, nor below, neither in sea,

Nor on shore, in skies above, Nor in the depths."

"You are the kernel of my heart,

You are the face of my sun,"

"You are the kernel of my heart,"

You are the face of my sun,"

"You are the harp of my music,

You are the crown of my company."

"You are the harp of my music,

You are the crown of my company."

SHE FELT a tear slide down her cheek. His voice was strong and sweet. He said the words just for her and she loved to hear his voice.

"Miss Glenna, take Sinclair's hand and repeat the vows after me."

She did as smoothly as she could, trying to express her love as clear as he had for her. As she spoke his smile grew and she knew he loved what he heard.

The pastor placed his bible in front of Hamish who placed two rings on the pages.

"These rings are given to signify the love you share. Sinclair give your ring to Glenna."

Sinclair picked up the ring and placed it on her finger. "This ring I give to you to show my love to you and to all."

"Miss Glenna, give your ring to Sinclair."

"This ring I give to you to show my love to you and to all."

They squeezed each other's hands. He placed her hand to his lips and kissed it.

"These two souls have found love through difficulty. But I know their love is pure. They have given their vows, and given each other rings, and I see no reason why I cannot declare them married."

She looked at Sinclair and he to her. They then looked at the stairs at his uncles who were smiling and nodding in agreement.

The pastor continued.

"Then in the front of these witnesses and in the sight of God and by the power of the Kirk of Scotland, I declare you are husband and wife. You may kiss your wife."

They came closer and gently kissed each other on the lips.

Hoorays and cheers echoed around them.

* * *

SHE WAS the most beautiful woman he had ever seen. Her mother's wedding dress hugged her as if it were made for her. From the first moment he had met Glenna, he had loved her and now he had married her. And in the foyer where he had returned to her only days before. The cheers and cries of joy were wonderful. He could not deny it but looking into her beautiful eyes and

161

seeing her gorgeous red hair laced with flowers, he knew he would be happy with his queen for the rest of his life. He was hugging her close and the family was all around them. And he could not be happier.

He placed her lightly bandaged hand in his and led her toward the dining room. The cheers and back slapping continued, and the joy filled his heart. Alasdair pulled out the seats for her and him and they sat down. Sinclair leaned toward her and whispered in her ear. "I love you. You have made me the happiest man in all of Scotland."

"That is convenient. As you have made me the happiest woman in all of Scotland."

He leaned in again and kissed her.

* * *

THE DINNER TO celebrate their marriage was wonderful. She could not have asked for a more delectable feast. Mrs Gillies had outdone herself. In twenty-four hours, cakes and sweet meats, dried fruits and baked goods covered the tables. Mead and scotch, tea and coffee, every drink she could imagine was present. A roast dinner of beef, chicken and veal was served with vegetables from all over the land.

Soon the speeches began. Dair did not disappoint.

"My sister has guided us through the fae world, helping us to acknowledge and accept our place in it. She has told us the stories, directed our paths, encouraged us to accept the love of others when offered to us." He took Molly's hand and drew it to his lips kissing her fingers. "Of course, I would want the same for her as she has helped to give to me and Molly, Duncan and Rachael and perhaps you one day, brother." He pointed to Hamish, who was gently shaking his head.

"So, I ask you to lift your glasses as we salute our dear Glenna."

Everyone did. "Slainte." Echoed through the room.

Hamish then stood.

"I met Sinclair just days ago, as most of us have, but he is an honourable man. His history and his family lineage would make most people sit up and take notice. But the thing which has impressed me most is his love and total commitment to Glenna. Welcome to the family 'Sin'."

Sinclair's laughter filled the air. "Thank you, 'Ham'." And everyone joined in the fun the two men were having with each other.

"Please raise your glass."

"Slainte."

Molly stood up. "I know it is not usual for the lady of the clan to say anything, but I wish to. Glenna, you are the greatest of friends. Sinclair, you have given Glenna great joy and love. May both of you live long and love forever." She too raised her glass and saluted the two loves.

"Slainte."

* * *

THEY HELD each other's hands as they walked around the rooms talking with all the guests. Though it was only a small affair all the clan and servants that were near came to celebrate their wedding. A table in the corner were covered in gifts. Sinclair could see bottles of whisky, food stuffs, fabric, clothing, boxes with secretly held items. Anything you could imagine seemed to be there.

He kept glancing at his beautiful wife and could see she was happy and excited but tired from all the events of the last few days. Perhaps now they had eaten and talked and danced and had fun it was time to retire to their room.

Hamish was suddenly at his side and whispered in his ear. "Time for you both to go."

Hamish stepped into the middle of the room. "Attention all, we have one more special thing to do before we let these love birds fly home to rest."

A small table was carried in by a footman and placed in the middle of the room. A maid placed three candles on the table. Alasdair came up to the table and lit the two outside candles leaving the one in the middle unlit.

Hamish continued. "I give you each a tapper. I want you to light the tapper on the candles that are burning and together light the candle that is unlit. As you can see one candle has the Murray tartan wrapped around it and the other has the Murray-Green tartan wrapped around it. When the new candle is lit you must then blow out the candle of your family tartan." The candle had no tartan.

Sinclair gently led her to the table, and they lit the tappers and their individual candle. Then then each blew out their family candle.

"My dear Glenna, and Sinclair, what you did not know was that you would become a new line of the Murray clan. In a few months I will bring to you a new tartan which will combine elements of your own clan tartans in a new tartan just for you. The Murray Murray clan."

Alasdair then said, "Farewell to you both. Go and rest."

All of them laughed and Alasdair gently guided them to the staircase.

"Now you will be escorted by Mrs. Boyce to a new room where your belongings have been placed. You are no longer entitled to separate rooms."

Everyone clapped and Sinclair took Glenna up the stairs. At the top, he picked her up in his arms and followed Mrs. Boyce. He could hear the voices from below, goodnights and whistles.

"Goodnight."

Some whistling and a big round of laughter.

"Hurrah!"

TOGETHER FOREVER

*A*t Last He walked into the room, and she was still in his arms. Her excitement grew. He placed her on her feet and thanked Mrs. Boyce for escorting them here. It was a guest room and had been decorated for them. Many of the flowers from the foyer were scattered around the room.

Sinclair closed the door and then locked it.

"Why did you lock it?"

"I don't want to be disturbed and I do not trust Hamish not to come running in at the wrong moment."

She laughed as he came and placed his arms around her.

"I have wanted you in my bed…our bed for so long and finally it is about to happen."

She leaned up and kissed him and deepened the kiss quickly. "I have wanted this too," she mumbled.

Without hesitation, he picked her up and carried her to the bed. She lay there as he came and laid next to her. He placed his hand on hers and then sat up.

"First, let me take these off you."

She sat up and he began to gently unwrap the bandages and

ribbon on her hands. He bought one naked hand to his lips and kissed her fingers.

"I wish this had never happened to you. I am sorry."

"It is not your fault. And Jake, sought my forgiveness. Which I gave. He was misguided and I forgive him."

"My sweet Glenna. You are wonderful to do that." He then gently unwrapped the other hand. Again, he kissed her finger when he was done. It felt like the most erotic thing he had ever done.

He kissed her and then kissed her neck and shoulders. He then got up and drew her to him. He turned her around and began to undo the buttons on her dress.

"You look beautiful in this dress. But please understand I want to see you out of it."

"I understand. As I want to see your beautiful body out of your clothes. Mind you, you look wonderful in a kilt. You will have to wear that again."

"Well Mrs. Murray-Green, your wish is about to come true. The taking off bit."

Before long they both stood there stark naked but so at ease. His body rippled as the warm air around him moved and she could feel every tingle in her breasts and around her private parts.

"You are the beautiful one. Your skin is so soft and smooth. I want to make love to you more than life itself."

"Then, my dear, take me to bed."

* * *

IT WAS STILL DARK when she woke wrapped in the arms of her beloved Sinclair. Never would she had thought that two people could be so in tune with each other. He had loved her over and over again, and it only got better. She had wanted this and now she knew they would be together forever. He was so caring and gentle but rough when she wanted him to be. They sailed in the sky. Well, that is what it felt like. Floating among the clouds tasting, loving, feeling each other as they floated in the air.

She chuckled to herself. She didn't know what it was like to float in the air, but she was convinced it was like making love.

"What's funny?" he asked.

"Us floating in the air. I was thinking it was like I was in the cloud when we made love."

He chuckled. "I was thinking the exact same thing. It would seem we think like each other, my dear."

"I am not complaining."

She turned around and faced him.

"I love you."

"And I you."

And he sent her to the heights of passion again and allowed her to float through the clouds with him.

* * *

THERE WAS a knock at the door, and she pulled herself out of bed and put on her dressing gown. Sinclair hardly moved. She went and opened the door. Her maid Jenny, blushing like a red rose entered with a tray of tea and coffee.

"What time is it, Jenny?"

"After ten, miss. I will be bringing you your breakfast shortly. I have strict instructions to keep you here all day."

"All day?"

"You are on your honeymoon, miss."

"Very well."

"I will arrange for all your meals to be brought here."

"Thank you, Jenny." Came the voice from the deep.

Glenna didn't think it was possible for Jenny to go even redder than she had, but she did.

Jenny placed the tray on the table and left.

Sinclair got out of bed and wrapped his dressing gown around him. But she had time to admire his fine figure and beautiful smile.

"Are you lusting after me, Mrs. Murray?"

"I am, Mr. Murray."

"Come, my dear, and have your tea."

She sauntered over to him and took his hand.

"Us together…"

"Is divine, my love."

They sat down and had their tea and coffee.

* * *

THE WHOLE DAY they locked themselves away, making love, sleeping and talking about the future, that looked so good to them both. This was all he had wanted. A Ghillies Dhu should never feel this way. Well, he might have been a Ghillies Dhu but no more. He was the head of his own little family. Not the head. He shared that position with Glenna. They were partners in every sense of the word. And members of a much bigger family of Murrays.

He stood near the window, looking out over the estate. He could see the forests stretching out to his left and the lake. The small hills rose in front of him. He had never owned land before. Though he did not own this land it would be part of his and Glenna's family for many years to come. He smiled, feeling a sense of pride and accomplishment. It would be his dream job to look after the land and trees in this beautiful estate.

He turned his head and saw Glenna walking towards him. She smiled, and his heart skipped a beat. He couldn't believe how lucky he was to have her in his life. Even to have a life with her in the past was better than a life without her. She was his best friend, his lover, and his soulmate.

He took her hand. They stood there, hand in hand, looking

out at the estate. He could see their future stretching out before them. It was bright and full of possibilities. He knew that nothing could stop them from having the wonderful life they wanted.

The fae world was at peace, Duncan and Rachael were together. Alasdair and Molly shared the fae blood as did he and Glenna. He could have insisted that he have the throne. He was a descendant after all. But he did not want it. He wanted Glenna and a future with her. A future in the past. What would the future hold? Only time will tell.

EPILOGUE

"Are you all right, my love?"

"I am more than all right." Her darling baby girl snuggled to her breast. She handed the baby to him.

Gently he cradled his little girl. "She has your hair and your eyes, darling."

"She is beautiful."

She watched Sinclair cradle her head and make cooing sounds to the babe. She had given him a girl. A fae to carry on their line.

Molly was sitting in the chair next to her bed with her own baby in her arms. Duncan Sen John Sinclair. He had fallen asleep once her baby had been born, apparently satisfied when everything had quietened down.

"What will you call her?" Molly asked.

Sinclair stood tall and proud.

"Annissa Maxine Murray Green."

"Oh, what beautiful names," Molly cooed.

Alasdair entered the room. "I agree, very nice." And he looked over Sinclair's shoulder at the little girl. "And as beautiful as her mother. Congratulations."

"And on this beautiful autumn day. Life is wonderful."

She smiled at everyone around her.

* * *

THE TEAL LIGHT was on fairy hill. It brightened and dimmed.

"All is well again. The fae world and the human world are at peace. I am glad you came and got me from the future. The Murrays are yet to know who I am exactly, but they will know one day."

"You are Queen Alvina. But there will a number of Alvinas in their history."

She laughed and he laughed with her. "But that, my dear Drake, is another story."

"It certainly is, your majesty."

And the light came and went, and they were gone.

FAMILY TREE

Murray Family

Duncan (Callum Malcolm Lucas)	⟷	Jean Louise Buchanan
Their children were:		
Duncan (Malcolm Peter Ross)	⟷	Rachael Fielding
Alasdair (Fergus John Peter)	⟷	Molly Grace
Hamish (Ross Callum Andrew)	⟷	?
Glenna (Jean Louise Mary)	⟷	Sinclair Murray-Green

Rachael and Duncan

↓

Clara Jean	Callum Duncan	Fergus Alasdair
2020	2023	2025

Malcolm Ross	Zola Grace	
Wallace Peter	2030	
2028 Twins		

Rachael & Duncan's children are born in the future in Scotland.

FAMILY TREE

Molly and Alasdair

Duncan Sen John Sinclair
1824
1826 Twins

Alvina Molly Jane Carina
1830

Lucas Brian Peter Ross
Jasper Alasdair Hamish Sen

Peter Duncan Stephen Giles
1834 *Known as 'Wee Peter'*

Glenna and Sinclair

Annissa Maxine
1824

Alvina Grace
1827

Rachael Jean
1828

Glenna May.
Rebecca Louise
1830 Twins

Maxen Ross
Timothy Sinclair
1833 Twins

Blake Peter
1835

ABOUT THE AUTHOR

Joanne loves to write, and she loves to travel. She is married to Andrew and lives in Central New South Wales Australia with him and their two cats Arthur and Oscar. (Meet them on Joanne's webpage) She has two grown sons and four beautiful grand-daughters. Her imagination loves to take her on various trips but mainly in the area of the regency romance.

She also loves meeting new people so do drop a line to her on:

Website Facebook Instagram Twitter

ACKNOWLEDGMENT

This was a hard final volume to write. Finishing a series can be difficult because you do not want to let go. The characters have been with me for many years and letting them go can be and has been very hard. The Murray clan have been an extra family for me, and I will miss them. I have included the family trees for each of the Murray siblings, allowing me to come and visit them again if I so desire. You might be satisfied to leave them here. But like me you might want to revisit the family some time. Let me know if you do.

I also want to acknowledge my local bookstore, The Book Connection. They have done so much for other local authors, and I want to thank them for all the promotions of my books that they have made. You guys are great, and I hope we can work together for many more years as I continue to tell my stories. Thanks for helping me become a popular novelist and a top selling one.

To all of you lovely readers who not only read my books but have connected to me personally to tell me what you have loved reading, I thank you. Thank you for bringing my books to others.

Lastly to two people who have been with me from the beginning. My editor, Nas Dean, and my cover designer, Danielle Hurps. You guys are the greatest.

FROM THE AUTHOR

I have loved using folk law and traditional history in this series. It has spurred my imagination. I love the way the fae have developed in the story and that they too are not perfect and can give a few bad apples to history.

Having mixed marriages was an idea which was there from the beginning but the fae blood would only appear in the females. That too was my idea and I loved playing with it.

If you loved the first 2 books, I hope you have loved Glenna's Future, the final in this series. And please tell your friends about this series.

Go to my website and subscribe to my newsletter. It is only monthly so you won't be bombarded by emails.

https://www.joanneaustenbrown.com/

or join me on my Facebook page.

https://www.facebook.com/joanne.boog/

ALWAYS ELSPETH (ALWAYS SERIES BOOK 2)

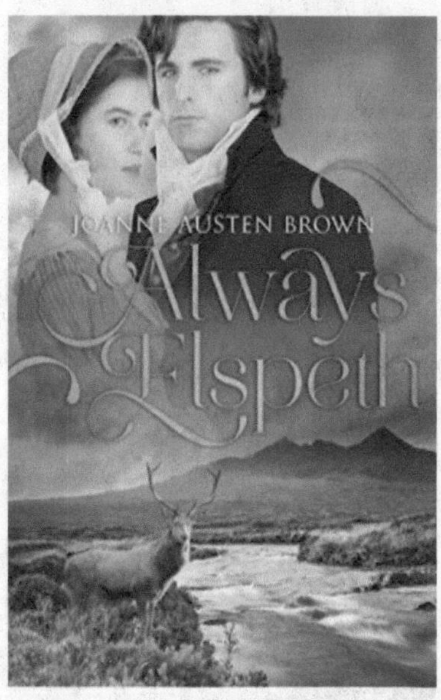

Tragedy has followed Elspeth. Hoping for a new life she moves to the Isle of Skye. Can the society that she hates leave her to start again? What she cannot see is someone who is following her.

James has loved her all his life. Elspeth rejected him once but now she may be tempted to try love again. But in the shadows, someone is stalking her.

Can James and Elspeth renew the love they once had? And make it stronger? Or will the darkness overtake them?

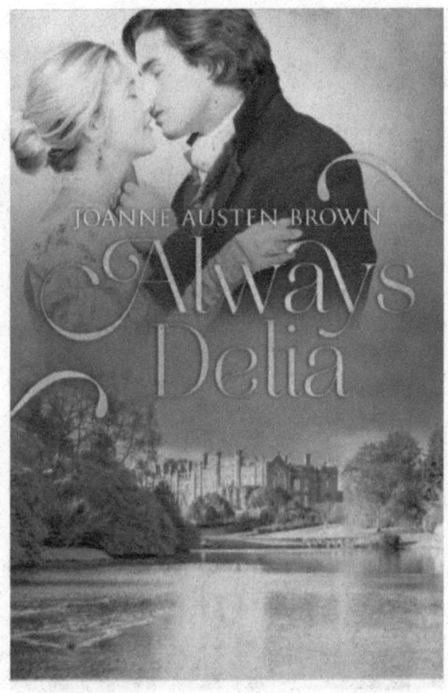

Delia has been in search for a man she believes is her real father. However, she has been unable to find him. Was her mother telling the truth? Delia decides to go home to the man who raised her and a brother who has protected her.

Lucas has loved Delia almost from the first moment they met. He has done all that he could to help her find her real father. But now he has, he wants to protect her from a man who he knows she will not want to meet.

Their families have been caught up in a twisted tale of love, loss, and villainy. Now they have a chance at real love and a happy ever after. Will it be for Delia and Lucas?

RACHAEL'S JAUNT (COME WITH ME BOOK 1)

Rachael Fielding loves Scotland. She escapes her busy life for some down time but does not expect that time to be in 1822. Is she dreaming? And why is the man she knows as her dream Scotsman suddenly there in front of her?

Duncan Murray is a laird though he does not want to be. But he was born to the position. Then Rachael shows up and his world is turned upside down. Can she be the love of his life and what have the Fae got to do with it?

Is she a spy for the soon to visit, King George 4th? Can he believe her stories of the future? The two will be tested to their limits. Will the Fae have their way and is there a future for Duncan and Rachael?

MOLLY'S LAIRD (COME WITH ME BOOK 2)

In her own time Molly is a fish out of water. But when she goes back in time to find some peace, after the deaths of all her family, she finds a new beginning.

Can all the promises of the past be true? What about the Fae? And can this handsome man be just for her?

Alasdair misses his brother but understands why he left. He is now Laird but is lonely. Will he find love like Duncan did? Who is the real Molly he cannot stop thinking of? Is she the answer to all he has been searching for? What are the Fae up to?

A PARTRIDGE IN HIS FAMILY TREE

Dianna Partridge rejected him, so he became a rake. But Jason Baird wants to settle down. He needs a woman not a simpering Miss.

Dianna has been running her father business, despite being a woman, and very well. But she feels she has missed out on some things.

Can these two get together and have a memorable Christmas?

Cora Fitzgibbon appears cold and uninteresting except To Thomas Wright.

He foolishly agrees to be part of a Secret Letter plan invented by his brother. Cold Cora is his match.

But she is not cold or distant and he is very much attracted to her. How can he win her love and keep his promise to his brother.

Love is in the air as Christmas approaches.

REDEMPTION

Hannah has faced to much sadness in her young life. Forced to marry an old man she did not love and say goodbye to the man she did love.

Timothy has to turn away from his Hannah and leave her to another, as he goes off to war. Can either of them find the love they want? What do they face? Can they be redeemed and find each other again? From the shadows of despair to the light of love. Theirs is a gripping tale of Redemption